what my last
man did

BLUE LIGHT BOOKS

The Blue Light Books Prize was founded by
Indiana Review and Indiana University Press
in 2015. This annual prize is awarded to an
outstanding short story collection or poetry
collection on alternating years.

what my last man did

ANDREA LEWIS

INDIANA UNIVERSITY PRESS
Bloomington and Indianapolis

BLUE LIGHT  BOOKS

INDIANA UNIVERSITY PRESS
Bloomington and Indianapolis

BLUE LIGHT BOOKS

This book is a publication of

Indiana University Press
Office of Scholarly Publishing
Herman B Wells Library 350
1320 East 10th Street
Bloomington, Indiana 47405 USA

iupress.indiana.edu

The paper used in this publication
meets the minimum requirements of
the American National Standard for
Information Sciences—Permanence
of Paper for Printed Library
Materials, ANSI Z39.48–1992.

Manufactured in the United
States of America

Cataloging information is available
from the Library of Congress.

ISBN 978-0-253-02670-5 (paperback)
ISBN 978-0-253-02676-7 (ebook)

1 2 3 4 5   22 21 20 19 18 17

for Deb

contents

what my last
man did

1

Tierra Blanca

I had what I wanted. I was alone with Charles. He was driving and I was so nervous I was tearing little pieces off the edges of his road map.

"The Spanish called it Tierra Blanca," he said. We were on New Mexico Highway 85, headed northwest out of Las Cruces. "But only one stratum is white."

Charles was a chemist. So was I, but he was the head of New Mexico State's chemistry department and I was a TA in freshman labs. Besides chemistry, he loved rare cactus, meteorology, and geology, including every rock he ever saw. "There's a fabulous collapse caldera up there, miles wide, filled with all kinds of pyroclastics."

I envied him these passions. If you had passions, you were living. Without them, you were watching—the way I was watching desert sand and half-dead creosote go by and wishing I'd stop craving attention from Charles.

I had met him three months before, when I interviewed for my job, buzzed on truck stop coffee, glazed doughnuts, and No-Dōz. I hadn't slept in two days, ever since I saw the job listing on a bulletin board at Rice. I called for the interview, packed my station wagon, went to Galveston and said goodbye to my mother and my sister Iris, both of whom pleaded with me not to leave, and drove nonstop from Galveston to Las Cruces. I changed clothes in a Texaco bathroom and went straight to Carmony Hall.

The door labeled "Dr. Charles Lancaster" was guarded by a secretary with huge tortoiseshell glasses frames and white correction fluid smudged on her cheek. Her nameplate said "Dorothy." I remembered her from my phone call.

She dragged her gaze up from the papers on her desk. "Name?"

"Hannah Delgado." I held out the single sheet of 28-lb ivory paper that was my résumé. "We spoke on the phone."

Dorothy took the sheet and dropped it on the blotter as though it were radioactive. "Applying for?"

"Lab instructor. I have an appointment. Remember?"

The door behind her opened and a tall man appeared. "Dottie? What's next?"

She leapt from her chair and almost bowed as she handed him my résumé.

His office was hot. Midday sun streamed through side windows, their sills crammed with plastic pots of cactus and two big chunks of purple crystals. His blue Oxford shirt had big sweat creases across the back. He was well over six feet, tan and fit, with a comfortable, rumpled look—messed-up brown hair and shoved-back shirtsleeves. I put him around forty-five and not handsome exactly, but striking because of his height and large head and thick forearms.

He pulled up two wooden chairs so they faced each other. When we sat down, our knees almost touched. While he glanced at my résumé, I studied the white squint lines embedded in the tan skin around his eyes. He looked up, smiling, and said, "My wife is giving me hell."

"Why?" I might've decided right there to fall in love with him.

"Because I put off these interviews for two months, and now the semester's about to start." He folded my résumé into quarters and leaned in, elbows on knees. "So. Hannah. Talk to me. Why should I hire you?"

He was sitting too close. A rapidly dissociating lime deodorant scent emanated from the open neck of his shirt. The blunt question, the physical closeness, the opening gambit "my wife," all demanded an intimate answer. What happened next was strange, but the whole eight-track of interview-speak that had looped through my brain since Galveston shunted to a forgotten section that contained the truth and I heard myself blurt, "My father died sixteen months ago. April tenth, 1974."

Charles straightened a little and tilted his head, as though he suddenly heard a baby cry deep in the woods.

Tears collected in my eyes. One rolled down my cheek when I blinked. He nodded, as if to affirm that crying was the one qualification he was looking for. I knew then I had the job, such as it was, with its poverty-line wage and the straight-faced imperative I would discover later in the *NMSUCD Lab Assistant Handbook* "to guide students in the proper techniques of the professional chemistry laboratory" and even "to write detailed and helpful correction-orientated notes" on their weekly lab reports.

He unfolded my résumé and scanned it again, perhaps seeking data that would explain my outburst. "I'm sorry about your father," he said. "You have other family?"

"That's the problem."

I did not mention the sinkhole that threatened to suck me back into Galveston. Did not mention my sister Iris or how she once pointed a Remington over/under shotgun at a flesh-colored Chrysler Newport full of developers my mother had invited to evaluate our land. Did not mention the financial setbacks my mother faced now that my father's businesses—opal mines, silver mines, nickel mines—proved to be a propped-up maze of illegalities. Did not mention Louis Paradiso, the faithful man who worked for us for twenty years and was now watching, bewildered, as our family and his life fell apart. Definitely did not mention Quentin Boudreau McKenna, III, who stood to inherit an oil fortune, small by Texas standards, but large enough to stem the rising tide of Mother's bad luck. My mother wanted me to marry him. *He* wanted me to marry him. Iris wanted me to do anything that would hold off the sale of our land. I wanted to get out of Galveston and start over.

A partially converted janitor supply closet in the basement of Carmony Hall became my office. The few books I had brought from Texas shared shelf space with boxes of brown paper towels that emitted the same alkaline aroma of defeat I remembered from junior-high bathrooms back home. Under the cataleptic flicker of fluorescent tubes, I graded lab notes at a primer-gray desk whenever I wasn't in the laboratory watching football-scholarship linebackers break beakers or stoned sorority sisters stare into Bunsen burner flames without blinking.

All the students—except one or two standouts who would've done fine without me—handed in lab reports that were at first shocking in their inaccuracies, then for a while hilarious, and finally depressing. I had been scrawling C-minuses and D's on quarterfinal tests when Charles stopped by my office that morning. He looked over my shoulder at the red slashes on the papers. "Ah," he said. "Our future Pasteurs."

"I showed them how to filter lead sulfate," I said. "I think they all left most of it in the filter paper."

"Maybe they were too dazzled by their instructor," he said.

I loved these compliments, which he lobbed at me like popcorn at a pigeon. I felt silly for craving his attention and powerful

What My Last Man Did

because he had noticed me. I bounced between those extremes, every other heartbeat, laying down hope one stratum at a time. The fact that he was all wrong—married, my boss, a flirt—gave me a perverse desire to make it right. Prove to some unseen audience—as if anyone were watching—that my considerable emotional and sexual powers, once unleashed upon the world outside Galveston, would be irresistible.

"All these Tertiary volcanic terrains up there." He was talking about Tierra Blanca, inviting me to go there that afternoon. I was wondering when I'd have the chance to kiss him.

We had been in the car for an hour. I had used that time to shred his map and hyperventilate.

"Along the river, you can see whole profiles of ash-flow tuffs, basalt, rhyolite." When Charles realized I didn't know what he was talking about, he added, "We'll see some fantastic views, too. Sunset, the Mogollons, everything."

My joy at having him to myself was chemically deteriorating into panic. I was afraid he would see how little of me actually existed. Afraid the pure New Mexico light pouring into the car from every angle would illuminate an outline of my body and the hollowness within. I wanted to catch him off-guard and blurt something crazy like, "What do you love most in the world?"

Without warning, Charles called out, "The open road," as if answering my question. "I could drive like this forever." He pointed at a wan streak of cloud on a horizon that seemed a million miles off. "Cirrostratus," he said. "Gorgeous."

My brain scrabbled like a gerbil in sawdust, looking for a way to match his enthusiasm. "It's beautiful," I said weakly. "It's so bright here. And dry."

"I forgot," Charles said. "You're from—where was it?"

"Galveston."

"Never been there."

"It's nothing like this. It's humid, it's hazy, it's lazy. I mean this kind of sun—" I waved my hand in a big arc, knocking my knuckle against the side window with a clunk. "This kind of sun feels like an interrogation. Like you better tell the truth all the time."

Charles laughed. "Were you planning on lying?" He turned off the highway onto a dusty strip of one-lane blacktop. "What's Galveston like?" he asked. "Sangria on the veranda? Mexican servants?"

He thought he was joking, but he wasn't far off. We did have a cook and a housekeeper, in addition to our all-around-everything man, Louis Paradiso, who seemed more like a benevolent uncle to me than a hired hand. "My family has a huge place there," I said. Then I worried that made us sound rich. "We used to be rich, but it all fell apart when my father died." I didn't want to talk about this. "I mean, the land's worth a lot. My mother wants to sell it. If she did, my sister Iris would probably kill herself."

"Really?"

"Well, she's distraught. She wanted me to stay and help her."

"And your mother?"

"She wanted me to marry this guy—"

"An arranged marriage?" He seemed to savor the possibilities. "Sounds medieval. Do you need to prove your virginity? Produce sons?"

The only man I had made love with was Quentin Boudreau McKenna, III, the heir to the oil fortune. We figured what-the-hell since our families were so keen on our union. He was very courtly, very gentlemanly, even as a teenager. We had been friends since we were five years old, playing games with Iris in our pecan orchard or looking for shark teeth on the beach. Whoever found a shark's tooth would close their eyes and make predictions. Iris always predicted Quentin Boudreau McKenna, III and I would marry. Ten years later, sex with Quentin was just another game. The hoped-for mingling of the families' DNA was our private joke, as we used double condoms and practiced what we thought were daring moves. I never dreamed he'd fall in love with me.

What My Last Man Did

The road curved, bringing low hills into view. They had white bands of sediment near their crests. Eager to change the subject, I asked, "Is that the ash-flow tuff?"

"Very good," Charles said. "The layer above it is called Gila Conglomerate." The strip of blacktop we had been driving on ended abruptly and became a dirt road.

I folded the map. My hands were shaking. Where were my irresistible powers? Why was I trying so hard to make an unavailable man like me? I felt sick with uncertainty, but knew I deserved misery for what I had done last week to Rudy.

Rudy was the Quantitative Analysis instructor who worked across the hall from me. One afternoon he had walked into my Chem 101 lab and asked me to dinner. There were students around, so I said "Sure," just to get rid of him. Rudy picked me up wearing a navy blue suit in ninety-degree heat. I had on shorts and a tie-dyed t-shirt because I assumed we were going for pizza or tacos. Instead we went to a steakhouse, a place Rudy probably could not afford, but where he had made a reservation. His sad efforts to impress me brought out a meanness I didn't know I possessed. I ordered the most expensive New York sirloin strip and complained about how it was done. I lolled in the leather banquette while Rudy spilled water, mispronounced Beaujolais, and struggled to spear limp lettuce with his fork. In minute detail, he described his dissertation on coupled clusters of mercury hydride. Even when he told me about his mother's death two months earlier, I couldn't muster much sympathy. As he dropped me off at my apartment, he asked me out again. I jumped from his car almost before it stopped moving and pretended not to hear.

Charles slowed as we passed a sign in the middle of nowhere that said "Gila Wilderness." He pointed again to the low cliffs. "The white outcrops are called Bloodgood Canyon Tuff. Of course the Spanish called it Tierra Blanca." Farther on, there was a parking area with a boarded-up Sani-Can at one end and an overflowing trash bin at the other. The smells merged mid-lot like a freak weather system.

Charles took a flashlight and a blanket from the trunk. As we climbed a steep trail he lectured on the welding of pyroclastic fragments and the formation of feldspar. He described the tuffs of Bloodgood Canyon which, over a few million years, had filled the collapse caldera. I was a pathetically willing student. If he wanted a woman who knew the difference between welded tuff and non-welded tuff, I would become that woman.

The top of the trail opened onto a flat stretch of pebbled ground above the Gila River. The light was kinder here. It was almost five o'clock and the afternoon sun slanted soft and gold from the west. A cool wind blew up from the river valley. We sat on the blanket near the edge of the bluff. The river traced silver curves below us, winding around yellow-green clusters of cottonwoods. On the opposite bluff, dark and light layers of basalt and sand were lit by the setting sun. I expected Charles to continue the geology lesson. Instead he touched my cheek and brushed back my hair. I was so grateful I leaned over and kissed him immediately, a little off-center and a little too hard. He pulled away and smiled. "Let's go real slow," he said. "That's how I like it."

I felt so foolish I almost cried. I lay back on the blanket and covered my face with my hands. "Well, not that slow," Charles said.

When he unbuttoned my blouse and started pulling it off my shoulders, I sat up and pressed my face into his chest. He had on a soft yellow polo shirt that smelled like Tide. I could've gone on breathing that scent for hours, but instead I grabbed the shirt on either side and pulled it over his head. His chest was very white compared to his tan arms. He sat there in his khaki slacks and I sat there in my shorts and pink bra.

When I looked at Charles's back framed against the blue sky it gave me a crazy impulse to make a wish—the way Iris and I would wish on things back in Galveston. Turtle eggs, meteors, seashells. Bring me a boyfriend, breasts, eternal love. I had an eerie sensation that Iris was watching us. She always seemed to know everything about me, sometimes before I did. When I was sixteen and snuck in after my first encounter with Quentin Boudreau McKenna, III, she sat up in the dark and said, "How was it?" She also seemed to know before I did how badly I would hurt Quentin. She used to say, "You're going to kill that boy."

We pulled off the rest of our clothes and Charles kissed me all over my body, even my feet. The cottonwoods below must have held a thousand cicadas; they thrummed along with us. Tierra Blanca seemed like a softly humming universe all its own. Finally Charles pulled me on top of him and kissed my mouth. He had a way of kissing that reminded me of Quentin. Was I destined to think of Quentin in every sexual encounter for the rest of my life?

When he entered me at last, it was so much better than the teenage practice sessions; it made me hope poor Quentin had found bliss somewhere too. I didn't do much except follow Charles's lead. I was too terrified to initiate anything or ask for anything or say anything. I moved with him, groaned with him, came with him, from sheer will to please.

Later, as we walked back in the near dark with Charles shining the flashlight on the trail, I relaxed for the first time all day. In the car, I wanted to talk, wanted Charles to pull off the road and grab me, wanted to drive all night until we reached Mexico, Honduras, Tierra del Fuego. But Charles hummed to himself and tapped the steering wheel as we sped down the dark highway. He had a green mask of dashboard light across his eyes. I remembered that same mask of light across Quentin's face the night he tried to give me an engagement ring. I did feel affection for him, his Cajun good looks, perfect olive skin and solemn mouth. We had driven to Freeport, where we sat in the car necking, looking at the Gulf, and talking. I knew I couldn't marry him.

"You seem like a brother, Quen." I pushed the ring back at him. "I'm sorry."

"Was the sex brotherly too?"

"Of course not."

"What if I beg you?"

"I just can't."

In truth, I wasn't sure why. I feared growing old in Galveston, having children with a man I used to play doctor with, having plenty of money but wondering forever what was over the horizon. The only Galveston person I missed was Louis Paradiso. I wanted the rest of them to leave me alone.

Quentin didn't give up. He even asked my mother and sister to help persuade me. That was when I saw the lab instructor job listing and ran.

* * *

The next day was Saturday and I had an afternoon lab. We were oxidizing copper with nitric acid and I needed to pay attention. But for most of the three hours, I was in a fog. When the lab ended, tables were strewn with dirty glassware, broken rubber stoppers, pieces of tubing, scraps of paper and copper plating, bottles of reagents, spills that could have been water or acid. The students were supposed to clean up, but there was a football game and everyone left in a hurry. I didn't care. I wanted an excuse to hang around in case Charles tried to find me.

I had just grabbed a broom when Rudy came in from across the hall. We had barely spoken since our stilted date at the steakhouse. Over his jeans and brown shirt Rudy wore a droopy lab coat with streaks of amber grime descending into the pockets on either side. He seemed not to notice he still had safety goggles on. He picked up the black wastebasket by the door and started sifting through the junk at the first lab station.

"You don't have to do that, Rudy."

He shrugged and tossed some scraps of rubber hose into the basket. He looked even more awkward than he did on our date. His hair—a mass of sandy curls—was bisected in back by the elastic band of his goggles. He had a big, shiny forehead, so broad that the rest of his face seemed to diminish under it to a dainty chin. He wore laced, brown leather wingtips. I wondered if he were the only man on campus, including 80-year-old professors emeriti, with shoes like that.

"Really, Rudy. You can go."

He held up a bottle labeled $HNO3$. "So, once again, we escape death and destruction at the hands of undergraduates."

I swiped debris from a table with my open hand—never a good idea—and felt the unmistakable pinpricks of glass.

"Damn." I looked at my palm. Five tiny specks of blood appeared where shards had pierced my skin.

When Rudy tried to look closely at my hand, he realized he was wearing the goggles. He blushed and took them off, raking some of his curly hair straight up from his bulging forehead.

"Ah. Surgery required." He grabbed the nearest first-aid kit and clanged open the metal lid.

"I can do it," I said.

He ignored me and took out a magnifying glass and tweezers. Even as he tugged out the first piece of glass, I watched the door and wondered if Charles would show up.

Rudy angled my hand into better light. "I wanted to thank you for being so kind the other night." He pulled another splinter out. "About my mother."

I tried to remember what I had said on our date about his mother's death.

"It meant a lot to me." He removed the last of the shards and rubbed my hand with a maternal touch. "I haven't told anyone else here about it." His eyes filled with tears.

"Believe me, I understand," I said. "My father died a year and a half ago."

"Oh—I'm sorry." He started to say more, but began crying instead, arms limp at his sides, shoulders shaking. For an awful moment I watched him, panic-stricken and guilty over how much I wanted Charles to appear and Rudy to get out. Finally, I put my arms lightly around him. He clutched me in a fierce embrace. "I'm such a wreck right now." He sniffed loudly into my ear. His lab coat smelled like sulfur.

At last he pulled away, embarrassed. His Adam's apple bobbed as he swallowed. "Want to do something tonight?" he asked. "There's a talk on uranium fission."

I looked at him, his raked-up hair and trembling chin and brown wingtips.

"I know," he said, "boring."

I kept looking past his shoulder at the doorway, expecting Charles to appear. But it was getting late. Charles was probably at home with his wife, dressing for an evening out.

"Okay," I said.

"I'll come by for you. Seven-thirty?"

"Okay."

Before I left, I went upstairs to Charles's office, hoping his secretary, Dorothy, wouldn't be there, but sure enough, there she sat, at 5:30 on Saturday afternoon, her smeary glasses making her look put-upon and angry.

"I was just wondering—" I rummaged in my bag as if I had papers for Charles.

"He's not here. I'll give it to him." She held out her hand.

"Never mind." I felt my face grow hot.

Dorothy removed her glasses and stood up. "The building's closed now." Of course that didn't apply to her. She probably lived there, guarding the door against girls who threw themselves at Charles.

I ran downstairs and outside. Charles was turning his car into his parking space in front of the building. We walked toward each other, but stopped an unnatural distance apart. "I thought I'd get here earlier," he said. "My wife had me at one of her charity things."

"I waited for you. I even went to your office. Risked having Dorothy kill me."

The gulf of sidewalk between us felt like an impenetrable barrier. Charles looked as if he would devour me if only he could cross it. "Are you walking home?" he asked.

"Yes."

"I'll take the car in a few minutes. I can be there soon."

I hurried home, wondering if I could find Rudy's phone number in the university directory. Wondering if I *had* a university directory. Wondering if I cared. When I unlocked my apartment door, the phone was ringing. It was Iris. Quentin Boudreau McKenna, III had been asking where I was, how to find me.

"Did you tell him?"

"Of course I told him," Iris said. "The poor boy is in agony."

"He'll get over it."

"You've got to talk to him at least. Even Louis says you should talk to him."

She would bring Louis Paradiso into it. The sure-fire way to get me to do anything. "Is Quentin going to call me?" I asked.

"No. He's coming there. To Las Cruces. I think he left earlier today."

"Iris."

"You should come back with him, Hannah. Whatever you're doing there, it's no good."

Through my front window, I saw Charles park and get out of his car. "I have to go now."

He came in and he closed the door and he pulled me to him. He kissed my neck and started undressing me. We dropped our clothes where we stood and fell on top of them. Charles was a lot wilder in lovemaking than he had been at Tierra Blanca. Maybe it was my irresistible powers. Again I had what I wanted. But now Quentin was in his little blue MG, probably doing ninety up state road 181 toward Las Cruces.

My apartment was hot. The sweat and the daring of being on the floor made everything sexier. Through most of it, I tried to banish images of Quentin proffering his poor diamond ring. Then Charles and I lay back, sated, but unwilling to move from the heat and exhaustion. Eventually Charles lifted up on one elbow and looked at me. "I can only stay another hour," he said. We started again, much more slowly.

Charles dozed afterward. When the knock on the door came, he startled awake.

"Who is that?" he whispered.

"I don't know."

A louder knock. Charles looked at me, puzzled. I shook my head as if mystified.

Rudy called my name once, twice.

"Is that Rudy?" Charles asked.

"I think so."

"Poor kid. He's probably madly in love with you."

I waited. Rudy's footsteps eventually faded away down the sidewalk. Charles fell asleep again and my arm was stuck somewhere under his ribcage. My hand went numb. Maybe he'd sleep beyond the next hour, get in trouble with his wife, divorce her, and marry me.

He snored softly for twenty minutes before the next knock came.

"Now what?" he mumbled.

I stayed curled against him and pretended to sleep.

Ann S Zaiman

Blue glasses
Write Carolyn

creosote

2

Rancho Cielito

Postcard

Only Louis Paradiso would send a postcard in a crisis.

Dear Hannah, it opens in his block-print hand. *I fear for the life of your sister Iris. She guards a nest and refuses food, even the filé gumbo she always loved, remember? Will you come? Louis P. April 30, 1976.*

I can see it now—the pelicans and their shit-smeared eggs, exposed and vulnerable in a messy nest on the muddy ground. Defying DDT, diving gulls, and developers. Depending on a few millimeters of calcium carbonate and Iris's protection to carry on the line.

I leave a note and skulk away on a hot Sunday afternoon. My job, which is hanging by a thread now that I'm no longer sleeping with my boss, will no doubt be terminated by the time I return. I drive my Ford Falcon station wagon from Las Cruces, New Mexico, to Galveston, Texas—reversing the trip I made just eight months ago—and arrive at 5 AM in front of our black grille security gate just as Louis unlocks it for a boxy yellow tractor fixed with a clay-caked bulldozer blade.

Louis

Most people, when they meet Louis Paradiso, assume he is Mexican. He often lets the misconception ride, but if you ask him, he'll ramble on forever about his heritage: octoroon prostitute grandmother from New Orleans, classical musician grandfather from the Austrian Empire, mentally unbalanced father of pure Chickasaw blood, and his beloved mother, Cate, who was fifteen and feral as a wildcat when Louis was born.

I don't remember the day my father hired Louis, but I know the story well, as it remained in Louis's repertory of morality tales taken from his life, the Bible, Jack London, and *Have Gun Will Travel*. I do remember evenings on the porch swing with Louis, the smells of mildew and DEET on the cotton cushions and Bugler tobacco from Louis's hand-rolled cigarette, listening to his gravelly voice, not caring that my sister was upstairs reading J. D. Salinger or making pencil drawings of an elephant beetle she trapped in a jar. I preferred the rectangle of stars above the porch rail and Louis's tales: the first time he bumbled down our driveway, gambled-out and hungover, and my father walked out of the rising sun *like Paladin down Main Street* and offered him—on the condition he stop drinking—the handyman job, beginning with Wheatena that morning and including meals and accommodation thereafter in the tiny apartment over the garage; or his grandmother Queen Juliette, who once owned a brothel in New Orleans called El Paradiso; or his mother Cate, who "lived high and died low," which was all he would say about her suicide. Louis adored her, even though she stuck the brothel name "Paradiso" on his birth certificate out of craziness induced by the early death of Louis's father.

In the twenty years he's worked for us, Louis Paradiso tended our land, repaired our house and turned himself into a minor legend on Galveston Island. He knows every tree in our pecan orchard, every anhinga in the freshwater pond, every palmetto, pepperbush, and Mexican plum along the driveway. He can read the weather from bruise-colored cumulus roiling up in the southeast or from a rustle of magnolia leaves in the yard. He can sense a freak blue norther when it's still in Kansas or a tropical storm when it's still off Florida. He had no family left, so he adopted ours. Before my father died, Louis helped him with his businesses, the semi-legitimate Bolivian silver mines, the Mexican sweatshops, the cousins and uncles who needed money, and the Gulf Coast shrimpers with chunks of opal hidden in the holds. He sang "Baton Rouge Blues" at my father's funeral, accompanying himself on his Fender Stratocaster. Louis Paradiso has always been the center strand in our family's frayed skein of love.

"One hundred dollars an hour," Louis tells me, cutting a glance at the plaid-shirt cowboy, who has his boots up in the tractor cab while he sucks slow drags on a cigarette. "It's a Fiat-Allis 16-B and the blade's a little too heavy for the job."

"Too heavy for what job, Louis?"

"Carrington can't have the money until the engineer says the land is okay. The engineer won't say the land is okay until everything's graded and he can fool around with his bullshit tests. He thinks Iris is out there to trick him."

Iris

My sister, Iris Benicia Delgado: at twenty-six, two years older than I am, but living in another century, the seventeenth perhaps.

Dropped out of Sam Houston High in the tenth grade because the teachers were "Philistines." Took up self-study of subjects she considered vital: natural history (specialty in Gulf birds), Southwest US history (specialty in Conquistadors), French literature (specialty in Georges Bataille), ecology (specialty in early eco-terrorism). Refuses to drive, refuses to eat or wear parts of animals, refuses to be wrong, and refuses to leave home even though our mother is trying to sell it out from under her.

Louis leads the way through the pecan orchard, which is dying from fungal leaf scorch, making it easy to glimpse our house through the stripped, black branches. My father, Ramiro Delgado, bought the place thirty years ago after he sailed home on the *SS Pretoria Castle* with his British bride, Carrington. It's always been called Rancho Cielito even though it's not a ranch. But the opulence of Rancho Cielito—its name, its mansion, its size and situation on the northwest coast of the island—was meant to show all of Galveston that Ramiro's branch of the Delgados were Mexicans to be reckoned with.

Still grand from a distance, the house sits like a dowager princess amid her fading court—encroaching salt marshes, some spindly yuccas and two morose magnolias in the yard. A deep veranda with eight brick archways runs the length of the front. Above that, two more stories of ivory stucco and red-framed windows, with improbable turrets at the top front corners. Terra rosa tiles from Oaxaca cover every peaked or curved or dormered roof section.

We come out of the orchard and start north across the flat four acres that run between the pecan trees and the hazy mangrove coast of Bayou Oviedo. Usually this ground is covered in crown vetch and St. Augustine turfgrass, but now the eastern half has been graded to a dried-mud crust, presumably by Plaid-Shirt and his Fiat-Allis 16-B. Louis avoids this section, as if the newly graded ground is contaminated or forbidden. Instead we walk through shin-deep yellow grass, still laden with dew. The sun is an ovate blob of ocher, stashed in one corner of the east. It looks squashed and bloated, too huge to overcome its ponderousness and rise much farther. Still, the heat of the day is gathering. Every few yards, a snowy plover startles up in a tan and white flapping arc, whistling a shrill *turrweet* and disappearing a few yards away. I can smell the low-water salt smell of the bayou.

As we near the mangrove marshes, the grass gives way to stubby fan palms and big clumps of asparagus fern. I don't see Iris until we're almost on top of her. She is sitting on the ground in front of a pathetic pup tent. She has marked a perimeter for her little camp by jamming broken sticks into the ground to make a circle maybe twenty feet across. She has binoculars around her neck, a fat black pencil behind her ear, a cloth-bound notebook in her lap. Propped on a little fake veneer table that I recognize as the nightstand from her bedroom is our old green Coleman jug with the copper spigot. At least she's still drinking water.

Behind the tent is the pelican nest, just as I pictured it: a low mound of wet dirt, hollowed down the middle and roughly outlined with a mess of twigs and feathers, reeds and refuse. In the center are two chalky-white eggs, each as large as my closed hand.

By way of greeting, Iris stands and asks, "What are you doing here?"

"Oh, nothing. I just came to watch Mother bulldoze you into the bayou."

She ignores me and turns to Louis. "What's happening up there?" Always thin, Iris looks emaciated now. Her legs are like soda straws in her baggy brown shorts and her shoulder points jut from her white sleeveless shirt. Her eyes, set back in bruised-looking sockets, are glittery and wild.

"Iris, honey, you have to come in. You have to eat." Louis pushes her tangled hair back from her face so lovingly I am reminded of our father, Ramiro. Iris and I adored Ramiro so passionately that for most of our lives we were locked in competition for the slightest sign of favor from him. He could be affectionate in small bursts, which we anticipated the way other kids might wait for Christmas morning, but mostly we loved him from afar. If he wasn't traveling or in Houston, he was working at home. Even the parties he and Mother gave were part of his career plan, going after politicians and con-men, socialites and celebrities. We never noticed, really, that Louis was our on-the-spot dad, the one who taught us how to roller skate, to name the birds and plants, to pick pecans. Yet he also seemed to be one of us kids. While we longed for our father, he longed for our mother.

Iris turns her face away from Louis's loving hand. "I thought you were going to stop her," she says, her voice trembling with fatigue. Only then do I hear a metallic clink and notice Iris has shackled her ankle to a Texas sabal, the chain snaking twenty feet away to the short, fat palm tree. As eco-terrorist measures go, it's a rather feeble chain. It reminds me of the kind that used to connect our tetherball to its pole.

"Sweetheart." Louis says, "It's your mother's land. I can't stop her."

"Yes you can. You and I are the only ones who care about it."

A shadow flickers and we all look up to see one of the pelicans circling overhead. It makes an angled glide toward us on its six-foot wingspan, flaps heavily to turn and climb a few feet before gliding round again. Iris tells us, "You have to leave. The mother won't come down with all these people." But the urge to protect the eggs is too strong. The pelican skids to a landing a few yards off and waddles up to her nest. She tilts her great, narrow head to look at us with one purplish eye, then climbs on top of the eggs, settling the heavy bulk of her dark brown body on the nest. After stretching once the long white S of her drainpipe neck, she folds it in on itself and rests her yardstick of a bill on her chest.

Iris turns back to me. "The babies will fledge in five weeks," she whispers. "Tell Carrington she can fuck it up for good after that. But not before."

What My Last Man Did

Carrington

Our mother, Carrington McAuley Delgado, must have looked very foreign indeed to Ramiro's family when she arrived here in 1949 with her pale skin and fair hair, her alligator shoes from Selfridges and her tailored, fawn-colored jackets from Kenneth Durwood of London. It didn't matter. She fit in like a long-lost sister with the entire Delgado clan, even the remote second cousins in Sinaloa and Jalisco, partly because she tried to speak Spanish, but mostly because she, like all of them, stood fast on one implacable value: family is everything. Not simply caring about family and loving family, not simply being prepared on holidays for however many of them might show up—prepared with dinner service for twenty-eight, walk-in freezers stocked with great shoulders of beef, linen closets stacked with Egyptian cotton sheets and Merino blankets from Cornwall, much too warm for Galveston, but so lovely—not simply accommodating family, but organizing family, governing them, really, through an invisible and relentless system of checks and balances, spies and manipulations, kindness and ruthlessness, in order to keep the entire organism healthy, aligned and functioning. In all these endeavors, Ramiro was the undisputed leader and Carrington was his first lieutenant. Family problems—alcoholic uncle, inappropriate fiancé, business failings, teen rebellion, ill-timed pregnancy, property disputes—were settled with anything from a raised eyebrow at Easter dinner to a lawyer with a bank draft in his breast pocket, but they were always settled by Ramiro and Carrington.

Two years ago this month, my father died on his Sea Ray fly-bridge cruiser in the middle of the Gulf of Mexico and the linchpin fell out of the Delgado dynasty. They scattered like tropical birds released from cages, free now to follow their repressed longings for autonomy, setting up minor fiefdoms on either side of the Texas border, happily engaging in disputes, power plays, fresh alliances and old acrimonies. Carrington, for all her good instincts, never knew, or never wanted to know, how much of Ramiro's wealth stemmed from shaky enterprises built around borrowed money, fickle politicians, and under-the-table agreements with family members and their friends. By the time she and Louis unraveled everything, paid the lawyers, paid the hush-money, and paid the indignant uncles and cousins, Carrington was left with Rancho Cielito, resentment, the always-stubborn Iris, and the ever-faithful Louis. I don't count myself in this equation, having fled to New Mexico, believing, as twenty-four-year-olds will, that I could leave them all behind and start my own life, which I've managed to botch fairly well to this point.

Louis and I go in through the kitchen, shadowy and cool. Heavy stockpots and fry pans hang from wrought-iron racks above the two big stoves. I breathe in the smells of my childhood: tortillas and onions, cilantro and jalapeño. Our family cook, Pilar, turns from one of the sinks and bursts into tears when she sees me, exclaiming in Spanish over how thin I am. She breaks three huge eggs into a copper bowl and whisks.

Through the dining room, past the gleaming cherry-wood table, across the Saltillo tile and Navajo rugs on the living room floor to the other side of the house where Ramiro's—now Carrington's—office occupies the front corner.

At six in the morning, my mother is dressed in a beige linen suit, her coral lipstick and brown eyebrow pencil carefully applied, her still-naturally-yellow hair in a short, curly cut. She sits straight up in Ramiro's black leather chair, talking on the telephone in her slow impeccable Spanish. Something makes me look at Louis. His whole face, maybe his whole body, changes in the presence of Carrington. I see his chest rise and fall in a deep breath. The papery skin around his eyes twitches. In an unconscious gesture, he rubs his palms against the sides of his work pants, doing what he can toward a hasty transition from hired hand to suitor of the mistress of the house.

My mother hangs up the phone and looks me up and down. "You're so skinny, Hannah. Have you fallen in love?"

The answer is yes, and miserably so, but I've never told her about the affair with the married man who is my boss.

"How can you leave Iris out there chained to a tree?" I ask.

"Darling, I haven't left Iris anywhere. She is there by her choice."

"But you could call this off."

Carrington rests her hands on the cracked leather desktop. In front of her fingers, arranged like a shrine, are an old photo of Ramiro in a silver frame, two red-carbon TWA airline tickets, and a pale aquamarine check from a Bahamian bank for 1.8 million dollars. Carrington, with her instinct for the dramatic, taps a short buffed nail on the check and says, "This is my life, Hannah, right here, my past and my future, condensed down to this."

"Don't be ridiculous," I say.

"She's not," Louis puts in with surprising force.

"Where are all your lawyers? That land doesn't have to be graded today."

"But it does," Carrington says. "It's a chain of command. It goes from Houston to New York to Frankfurt. Interest rates change, you know. Currency fluctuates. They say, 'Finalize the sale or cancel it.' They can always build their resort somewhere else."

"So let them."

Carrington holds up the check. "And trade this for two pelican eggs?"

"Daddy would." I'm not sure this is true, but Ramiro did occasionally have a flair for championing the underdog. "He'd at least call their bluff."

Carrington looks at the black-and-white picture in the silver frame: Ramiro, age thirty. He's wearing a loose white muslin shirt and has a thick dark moustache. He stands next to a short Mexican fan palm and one succulent frond bisects his chest. With his heavy eyelids and satiny dark skin, he could be a jungle cat that is almost asleep or about to kill an antelope. This two-sidedness was always what made him so attractive. But Carrington's slit-eyed gaze at the photo makes me realize how betrayed she feels.

"Carrie," Louis says. The word hangs there—the first time I've heard Louis call my mother anything but Mrs. Delgado. All the roles rearrange. I realize how far it's gone between them and who will be with my mother on TWA. I was so naïve; I had thought the other ticket was for Iris. My mother lets it sink in. Louis waits for my reaction. I'm too proud to give them one. Instead I return to the kitchen for my breakfast.

Pelicans

After Pilar stuffs me with huevos rancheros, tortillas, sliced peaches, and a reheated chili relleno she found in the fridge, I fall asleep on the porch swing for a few hours and wake up hot and disoriented. The heat of Galveston hits me as a thing measured more in memories than in degrees. Whenever I come home I find myself gauging heat and humidity by how much childhood grief they churn up. I never manage to separate the measurable from the immeasurable, the atmospheric from the melodramatic, the actual density of the air from the scents and sounds and sights it carries. The cicadas are my mother telling me to make up my mind. The cloud streets—high bands of cumulus stretching to the sea—are Louis and the way he loved us when we weren't looking. Honeysuckle is the hum of bees, which in turn is Iris screaming she'd been stung. Her cries were so maniacal they brought my father to the porch with a shotgun. But it was Louis who dressed the wound. The damp packed earth beneath the magnolias was our playground, but even when I was small I watched the middle distance, as if my destiny might arise from the grooved line where the mangroves met the sky. Sometimes a pelican would appear out of the haze, six horizontal feet of pterodactyl in an effortless glissade, cruising just above the treetops, riding down the long, drawn-out minutes of the morning.

I walk back out to Iris's camp. Both pelican parents are in attendance now. The father struts back and forth on his black webbed feet, policing the perimeter of the nest. The mother still rests on the eggs. The two of them exchange low throaty noises and occasionally spread their vast wings almost in anger, but they resettle companionably.

Iris is asleep inside the pup tent, lying flat on top of a sleeping bag, her mouth open. When she wakes up I ask her what's with the chain. "Louis could probably break that with his bare hands," I say.

"I know," she admits. "I wanted them to see I was serious." She sits next to me on the ground, and I feel like we are back at Brownie camp.

"Look. Why don't you come to Las Cruces with me? You'll have to pass on the pelicans, but the place is rife with Conquistadors."

Iris begins to cry. She never was much of a crier, so I figure it must be the hunger breaking her down. "How long since you've eaten?"

"I don't know. A week." She sniffs.

I put my arm around her, but it's too hot and sticky so I drop it. "Are there any more nesting pairs now? Since the ban?" DDT, which weakened pelican eggshells, was banned four years ago. Since then, Iris and a few thousand other Gulf Coast birders have been praying for a pelican comeback.

"This makes three on the island." Iris scratches at a puffy red mosquito bite on her arm. "The same day I discovered this nest she told me she was selling everything."

"Has anyone been out?" Sometimes a state or university naturalist will come to gauge the porosity of the shells.

"No. They're all in love with Louisiana right now." Iris twists the clamp she has rigged around her ankle. The only clean spot on her bare leg is where the shackle has rubbed the dirt off in a pinkish white ring. "Anyway, it isn't just that. All kinds of crappy stuff will get built here and crappy people will come and dump their crap all over, and then what happens to all the animals?"

With a few soft squawks, the pelican parents trade places. The male climbs on the nest and covers the eggs with his broad feet. The female mutters what sound like instructions to him before lifting off and flapping hard toward the Gulf.

"I think she's still mad at Daddy for dying," I say. "She feels like she doesn't have a choice. There's not much cash left."

"She could live here forever. She wouldn't have to do anything. Louis and I would take care of the place."

"I don't think you can count on Louis anymore."

"Why not?"

At the same moment it dawns on Iris she has no allies left we see Louis and Carrington come out of the pecan orchard and start across the turfgrass. The tractor takes a longer route on the road, but I hear it coming too. Louis carries something in his left hand. I finally make out the long-handled bolt cutters. Carrington is still in her beige suit, complete with jacket, but she has put on short yellow rubber boots.

Neither of them will look at us as they tromp through the field. Louis squints at the horizon. Mother keeps looking over her shoulder for the tractor.

Louis says nothing as he approaches, stoops down, and cuts the chain. After he cuts it, he busies himself with unhooking and collecting loops of chain from around the sabal.

Iris sits, eyes closed. The tractor has begun grading the field on the far side. The low whine of the engine rises and falls as Plaid-Shirt shifts gears. The bulldozer blade methodically pushes heaps of dirt and grass forward and off to the side.

To my surprise, Carrington sits next to Iris on the muddy ground in her beige suit. She tries to take Iris's hands. Iris pulls them back and hides them in her armpits.

"I'm sorry, Iris."

"No you're not." She sounds about four years old.

The tractor grinds to within fifty feet of the little camp, uprooting the first of the fan palms and shoving them aside like toys. It stops and backs up for another pass. The noise unnerves the male pelican. He flaps and lifts off the nest. The panicked female returns with a clumsy landing. They both waddle about furiously and tilt their long curved heads at the eggs. The mother climbs back on the nest.

"It's my fault," Carrington says. "I didn't watch out for what Ramiro was doing. I trusted him too much. I loved him too much."

The tractor approaches again. The whine of the engine sounds different this time. I realize the difference is Iris emitting a sound that is part moan and part scream. This keening rises and sustains itself, seemingly without a breath for an endless minute, maybe two. Carrington leans closer, her head almost on Iris's chest, as if to absorb some of this grief. When it ends, she and Louis, one on either side, try to gather Iris up and lead her off. Iris twists and jerks her way out of their grasp, all sharp elbows and tangled hair. For some reason, she grabs the water jug and holds it in front of her like a shield. Trying for a proud, defiant walk and trailing a short length of the broken silver chain, she goes to stand in front of the nest. But something about the way she purses her lips—just the way she would when she was losing at Monopoly—tells me she knows it's over.

The bulldozer blade scrapes closer to the camp, which now looks like something abandoned by kids who slept outside on a lark. It stops again and Plaid-Shirt, expressionless behind mirror sunglasses, sits in the cab over the idling engine, waiting for a sign from Carrington. Carrington gives a sign, but it is to Louis. Louis gently takes Iris's arm. With his other hand, he again pushes hair from her face. He says something into her ear. In response, she tries to hit him in the stomach with the water jug. Louis picks her up and carries her to the side.

Carrington points at the tractor. Plaid-Shirt works the lever to lower the dozer and more earth folds and buckles before the blade. The little perimeter of sticks that Iris planted is scattered and plowed under. The tent canvas twists beneath the concave blade, the nightstand rolls over and breaks apart. Everything is scraped aside along with big clots of grass, their network of root threads turned to the sky. As the tractor closes in on the nest, the male pelican flaps up and down in high, frantic hops, squawking above the engine noise. I can feel the gritty air stirred up by his immense wings. The mother sits as long as she can, stretching her neck out to its longest length and coiling it back. Finally she staggers backward off the nest, emitting shriek after shriek of high-pitched anguish.

With surprising accuracy, Iris throws the Coleman jug at the tractor. It dinks off one wheel cover. Both pelicans lift off heavily in a low flight toward the mangroves as the blade flattens the nest. The eggs roll off, only to be quickly plowed under by the mound of earth building behind them. Plaid-Shirt throws it in reverse. The jug is flattened under a tire as he backs up. Both birds return immediately and land. They waddle across the sterile square yard of earth that held the nest, tilting their heads as if the eggs might reappear if they can get the focus right. The tractor moves in again and the two pelicans, after a wobbly running start, flap hard and fly, much higher this time, into the humid haze over the mangroves.

Queen Juliette

Iris never spoke to Carrington again. She wanted never to go into the house again, but she had to rescue hundreds of books and file folders from her room upstairs. She had to rescue the twenty-pound Underwood typewriter with the aqua-green keys, her antique Zeiss-Ikon binoculars, her *Sibley's Birds of the South Gulf Coast*, her Leica with all its telephoto lenses packed in foam-lined metal cases, and the eight-volume leather-bound set of Conquistador chronicles she stole two years ago from the City Library of

Houston's Special Collections. She had to rescue books in French, books in Spanish and huge art-photography books in German, which wasn't even one of her languages. She had to rescue files with labels like "Anhinga, juvenile plumage" or "Coronado/syphilis" or "Cichoriaceous plants/TX & LA."

When she realized Louis had moved out of the garage apartment and into the house, Iris carried every box of books and armload of folders herself, down the curved mahogany staircase, across the driveway and up the rusty metal stairs to the apartment. She refused to let me help, even though she was down to 97 pounds after her hunger strike. In the apartment, she reshuffled and repacked everything according to an organizational voodoo only she could comprehend. Then she decided to move back to Las Cruces with me, so it all had to be carried back down the metal stairs to my car. I rented the smallest U-haul I could find, hoping the Falcon could still move with the weight of Iris's life and fury hitched behind it.

Over those last few days, I'm not sure Iris ever slept. She was in a fever of obsession—eyes crazy-bright, forehead shiny—protecting and preserving her possessions. She rarely stopped moving except when some beloved book caught her attention. Then she'd sit cross-legged on the floor, engrossed in its pages for a minute or an hour before springing back up with new, frenetic energy. She was eating again, but she never finished anything. Little crusted-up, half-full bowls of applesauce or limp Sugar Frosted Flakes in separated milk lay all around the apartment.

Except for Iris's clutter, the place still held the few furnishings Louis had collected over the years: single bed, two threadbare easy chairs, a little table. He also left behind his four most prized possessions. I could understand why he left them. To be with my mother, it helped to leave your prized possessions or your ego or your essence elsewhere. So Louis's blue metal-flake Fender guitar was still propped against the windowsill that held the Sitting Liberty silver dollar Ramiro gave him as his first day's wage, a blue-and-white checkered poker chip from the Crystal Palace Casino that he often said reminded him of his checkered past, and his grandmother's small ivory pelican with its black-dot eyes.

The night before we left, Louis came to say goodbye. It was dusk. The only light in the room was Louis's ancient brass floor lamp with the coral paper shade. Iris sat in its circle of light, reading. I was half asleep in the other chair. Without saying anything, Louis went to the windowsill. I thought he was going to claim his prized possessions after all, but he turned and looked at Iris with a sad pleading of fatherly love. For her part, Iris clapped shut her copy of *Le Bleu du ciel* and glared at him. His chest in its pressed white shirt rose and fell in shallow breaths. He picked up the little pelican. It was only three or four inches of polished ivory, not even carved in much detail, but the long flat bill had a realistic sepia tinge and the eyes, just tiny dots, were expertly placed.

"Remember where this came from?" He knew we remembered, but that never stopped Louis from telling a story. "This belonged to my grandmother, Queen Juliette. Remember?"

"I remember she was a whore," Iris said.

Louis bowed his head over the carving. "True," he said. "But her father sold her into that life. She was only fourteen."

"Another happy, nuclear family," Iris said.

He turned it over in his palm. "This was the only thing Juliette had from her own mother. Folks believed a mother pelican would feed her young with her own blood if necessary."

"I'm touched." Iris reopened her book and pretended to read.

Louis went on. "My grandmother did all right though. She made a fortune."

"What happened to it?" Iris snapped off the question without looking up. She knew that this part of the story tortured Louis.

"Well, my mother Cate got it." Louis tried to laugh a little, I think to keep from crying. "But she lost it all."

"Mothers are funny that way," Iris said.

"I forgave her, Iris. She couldn't do anything right, but I loved her."

Louis held out the pelican and took two steps toward Iris. She dragged her gaze up from *Le Bleu du ciel* and fixed him with a look of bored hatred.

"Take it, Iris," I said. They both jumped a little, having forgotten I was there.

"No," she said.

"Just keep it for me." Louis held it under the coral light. The polished ivory shone and revealed its fine network of pinkish brown veins.

"Why?"

"Take it on loan," Louis said. "From Queen Juliette. She was smart, Iris, and brave. Like you."

"I don't want it," Iris said. But as if her hand couldn't obey her voice, she reached up and took it. She held it by its little ivory feet and looked it in the eye.

3

Queen Juliette

10 February 1895

> Maestro Rainer von Schofeld
> Chartres Street at Dumaine
> New Orleans, Louisiana

Francesca Countess von Schofeld
Neustadtviertel, Linz
Empire of Austria

Dear Mother,

Please stop worrying about my search for a bride. The day I arrived here, patrons of the French Opera House began flinging girls at my feet. They cannot bear for their new maestro to be *sans* female companionship. Even if said maestro does stand a mere five and a half feet tall and have rather too high a forehead and too thick an Austrian accent. ("He is thirty-three? And unmarried?")

Case in point: dinner Thursday last at Phillip Gerrity's—his fortune made in canals and bridges, his townhouse tucked into the elite Lower Garden District, his wife's taste running to massive pieces of Hepplewhite decked out with paisleys, brocades, gewgaws, and froufrou.

His wife paraded their daughter before me like a veal calf on market day. Seraphina Carolina Kincaid Gerrity. A lovely child, perhaps eighteen, overdressed and nervous under the ferret gaze of her mother. Mounds of alabaster flesh on display. The girl's pink frock was so puffy she threatened to levitate to the punched-tin ceiling. She had pleasing green eyes and shot me the occasional mischievous glance. While my first thought was *Frederick should meet this girl*, I did find myself attracted.

After a tedious supper, Mrs. Gerrity pushed Seraphina to the pianoforte. So many of these ladies imagine music is the way to my heart. Seraphina, to her credit, kept it short, singing a Liszt setting of *Die Stille Wasserrose*, and not badly, but she perspired so freely I took pity and asked if she'd care to walk outside. Her mother pounced on this request and herded us out the door. We walked under their magnificent oaks and I attempted conversation, but Seraphina preferred kissing. I admit I obliged her. When I asked if she'd be home in the coming week, she said, "All the time. Or I could come to you." So you see, Mutti, American girls are bold and opportunities are boundless.

Please forgive me for leaving Magda behind in Vienna. I know you wished us married, but we are not suited in the least. I trust she was not truly broken-hearted—you know what a great actress she is. Anyway, why cannot she marry Frederick? We look somewhat alike but he is taller and if you had one son married, you could suspend half your despair.

All my affection,
Your son, Rainer

2 April 1895

Dear Mother,

To answer your questions: yes, I have spent time with Seraphina and yes, she is a sweet and wholesome girl and yes, she is interested in marriage. Her coterie—spoiled daughters of the Garden District and their obedient beaux—have kept me entertained with their idea of the high life. I've drunk cognac and Bordeaux, eaten foie gras and frog legs, sat under magnolias and mimosas to sip juleps or ginger beer, smoked excellent LaGloria Cubana Minutos and taken breezy lakeside rides in handsome phaetons, all with Seraphina stuck like stickleweed to my side, arrayed in elaborate frocks from blinding white to devil red. I could propose now, but why spoil the sport of watching her win me? Given the hours of rehearsal at the Opera House, including harangues from the house manager and mishaps from wardrobe, diversion with Seraphina is always welcome.

Seraphina's parents—her father forever puffing on a Meerschaum and her mother forever eyeing the social ladder—are the quintessential parvenu opera patrons, attending every performance and contributing tidy sums. In fact, this whole city is mad for opera. Bootblacks whistle "Una furtiva lagrima" in the streets! Waffle men, clothespole men, fig men, and icemen sing out their wares in the most astounding voices. People of every race, caste, and hue come to the opera house, with coloreds seated or standing one or two balconies up, darkest skins farthest from the stage. The zeal of the audiences compensates for the poor lighting, the moldy walls, and the crushing humidity, which takes entire string sections out of tune in ten minutes.

What My Last Man Did

My debut production—"The Daughter of the Regiment"—was well-received. Our star tenor drank like a Spanish pirate, yet his voice held and he never missed a cue. One night a piece of château fell on a soldier and gashed his forehead, but he kept singing. Everyone loved it. To add to the drama, there was a race riot in the city during the final performance. These riots break out like thunderstorms—violent and fleeting—usually over labor problems. Negroes taking jobs, Negroes refusing jobs, Negroes wanting higher wages, and hooligans opposing them. We were forced to remain in the opera house until the disturbance abated. Made me feel I was living on the Wild Frontier. Don't worry—I am quite safe.

Your devoted (bachelor) son, Rainer

10 April 1895

Frederick von Schofeld
Neustadtviertel, Linz

Dear Frederick,

Thank you, Little Brother, for your letter with its leering references to my new "fiancée." You know perfectly well I have not proposed to Seraphina, nor done any of the things to which you so cleverly and glancingly refer. But my life here is not entirely dull. I haven't told Mother everything. In fact, thanks to the race riot I mentioned in my last letter, I have met an intriguing creature.

Because we were barred that night from leaving the opera house until 2 AM, all the performers, dressers, ushers, and audiences—even those from the colored balconies—gathered on the main floor. A rare but propitious co-mingling of social strata and pigmentation. We handed round champagne and the mood turned festive.

One striking girl glided by, so tall that the entire assembly gaped at her, yet so beautiful no one dared approach. She had a startled gazelle quality, sleek and vulnerable. Only a maid accompanied her, so I introduced myself and we conversed. We must have been quite a spectacle: the elfin maestro and his long-stemmed *fleur*. She wore a glistening aquamarine gown that frothed about her like the glacial waters of the Alps. All the so-called European ladies (that is to say, no African blood) regarded her with jealousy and loathing. Yes, she is colored, Frederick—are you shocked?—but nothing like the obsidian-hued Africans we have glimpsed in the capitals of Europe. She is probably a quadroon or an octoroon, as they say here. They are a caste called "free people of color" (first balcony). To envision her skin, think of Arabian coffee laced with crème fraîche.

Her presence transformed me so that I almost felt handsome, like you, as I gazed upon her. Her skin actually *shone*—I can't explain it. I understand there is a cream women use containing crushed pearls. Could that be it? Her eyes were long and slanted, and her hands, in ivory gloves, were slender and expressive. No more than twenty years old, yet she had read the entire libretto of "Daughter" and expressed great sympathy for the abandoned girl, Marie.

I discovered her name at least—Julie Devereaux—but she slipped away before I learned anything about how to find her. Now I am frantic to see her again.

Impart none of this to Mother, Freddi, please! She is still upset over my leaving Magda and still hoping I'll marry Seraphina. If she knew I was lusting after an African, she would disown me. You have much more experience than I with these matters. Send advice!

Your clumsy older brother, R.

1 May 1895

Dear Mother,

Magda is in New Orleans! Did you know this? She arrived last week on the *E.H. Fairchilds* from Memphis. Half the men of Austria at her feet, and she traipses after me! She burst into the opera house on Wednesday afternoon, wearing the pointiest shoes, the biggest bustle and the reddest rouged lips I've ever seen. She brought the entire rehearsal of "Robert le diable" to a standstill, greeting me like some long-lost intimate, trailing a flea-bitten greyhound on a leash and bossing about a poor mulatta. She probably kidnapped both on the docks.

Using all the false charm for which she is famous, she has coerced the poof who runs the St. Charles Theatre into giving her the lead in one of those overwrought Sardou melodramas in which she fancies herself the next Bernhardt.

First she insists she is not in New Orleans for *me* (merely "touring the colonies"); then she gads about with her theatre friends, hinting at romance between us. The gossip-starved newspapers eat it up—*ah, the charming rumor, ah, the Maestro and the Actress, a little bird told us,* etc. Last night she invited me to supper. Luckily I had an engagement with Seraphina, which was tedious enough—two hours of St. Michael's church choir mangling Bach—but was preferable to Magda's histrionics.

SAME DAY. LATER—This afternoon Magda arrived uninvited at my apartments, bearing a box of cigars and a silly glass parrot on a stick. She claims they are peace offerings and we should remain friends, or *camarades*, as she likes to say. But I want nothing to do with her. Seraphina, since seeing rumors of Magda and me in the newspapers, has sulked in a snit of jealousy. She said she would *murder* Magda. A sweet girl from the Garden District talking of *murder*. That's the kind of mayhem Magda stirs up everywhere she goes.

Mother, Magda trusts you. Please send her a letter and reason with her. Convince her to quit New Orleans and return to Vienna. I beg you.

Rainer

17 May 1895

Dear Frederick,

Truly, Little Brother, you are wasting your time in Linz. Come to New Orleans. We need engineers here, too. Dykes, levees, depots, piers, docks, bridges, buildings—all are either going up or coming down at a rate we never witness in the Old World. And there are amusements aplenty—you could maintain your Frederick-the-Rake reputation, drink and debauch till dawn, and then build a castle or courthouse by teatime.

Allow me to recount an evening I spent with my brass section on their latest carousal through "the District." I was supposed to be at Seraphina's whist party but left early in search of darker adventures.

René H. (trombonist) had procured a copy of *The Mascot*, the catalogue of concupiscence that guides gents through the strumpet-maze of Storyville and beyond. He devised an itinerary of saturnalia that would have pleased even you: first, Miss Ray Owens' "Star Mansion" on Iberville, where an engauzed girl attempted an Arabian seven-veils dance to music by a blind harmonium player; next, Miss Antonia P. Gonzales on Villere Street, where Antonia herself plays the cornet, albeit fully dressed and, one assumes, fully sighted; next, "The Phoenix," featuring a circus of Negro midgets performing lewd acts. Of course, all these staged tableaux are mere sideshows to the ladies of the night employed at each establishment. I had no intention of availing myself of their charms, however tempting some may appear in *The Mascot*. Gonorrhea ("the gleet") and syphilis ("606") are rife here. René H. tells me the girls massage a man's member with potassium permanganate to protect against contagion. Apparently the penis turns purple as a petunia.

Our final destination was "El Paradiso," the highest-priced bagnio on Basin Street, where the promised star octoroon goes by the name Queen Juliette. We arrived at two in the morning and I, unlike my brass section, was tired of the whole adventure. But I was mildly drunk on watered-down rye whiskey and let myself be dragged in.

Imagine my amazement when I learned the aforementioned "Queen Juliette" is none other than Julie Devereaux, the ravishingly beautiful, unforgivably tall octoroon girl I met the night of the race riot. I rushed to speak with her, but, alas, she was otherwise engaged. I learned that one arranges far in advance for an evening with Queen Juliette. I asked the Madam—a turbaned St. Domingue Negress the size of a small cottage—if I would be allowed to invite Queen Juliette to be my guest at the opera. The woman took charge of the affair like a Leipzig lawyer. She cogitated every detail—such as the size and condition of the carriage that would transport her prime chattel six blocks to the opera house—but the evening is fixed: June 3, for the second performance of "Robert le diable." I am brainsick with anticipation.

Freddi, this Juliette is as tall as René H., so at least six feet. Can you picture the two of us? I cannot tell you how exquisite she is, like a delicate animal, feral and sublime. She was wearing a white messaline robe that clung to her body like integument and flowed behind her like ice, and her feet were bare! Which proved somehow more provocative than all the décolletage, veil dances, and naked midgets on parade to that point.

Am I intrigued merely by her African blood? Do you think it is safe to consort with them? It feels like school days, when the more forbidden something was—first sweets, later smoking, then liquor—the more we wanted it. Is she forbidden because she is beautiful? Because she is African? Because she is a demimondaine?

I left El Paradiso and walked to the foot of Esplanade and hurried across the French Market—you should smell it at night—rotting fruit, rancid shrimp vats, trampled flowers—along the river to my apartments on Chartres, wondering how I would keep knowledge of my beautiful opera guest from Seraphina and her parents. In truth, I should break it off with Seraphina. Only cowardice keeps me trailing about with her. I am quite bored. She was angered by rumors of Magda and me in the newspapers. If only she knew no threat comes from that quarter but from the salacious parlors of Storyville. Remember, nothing to Mother.

Rhine

27 May 1895

Dear Mother,

I continue to pray that Magda will receive a letter from you. An unfortunate incident occurred Friday noontime in my parlor. Magda stopped here on the pretense that her mulatta had run off with a French gunrunner and that she—Magda—had to dress herself. *Quelle horreur.* She pretended to need buttoning and then, as soon as my hands touched her gown, flung herself onto my person. Naturally, Seraphina chose this moment to arrive for our walk.

Mother, Seraphina is a healthy, well-built girl. She pulled Magda off me as if plucking a pomegranate from a branch. She called Magda names I never dreamed she knew. She picked up the glass parrot—rightly guessing it was from Madga—and dashed it to the floor. It shattered into a thousand colorful shards, one of which she brandished close to Madga's face. Well, you know how fearful Magda is of her beauty, her coin upon the stage. She struggled and Seraphina flailed away, slashing violently enough to rip Magda's sleeve and pierce the skin. A little blood beaded up, but it wasn't a deep cut. Magda pulled free and fled. I would have gone after her, but Seraphina turned on me! She still gripped the glass and she demanded to know when we'd be wed.

It sounds like the kind of thing Frederick would be involved in. Should I have proposed to her under threat? To calm her, I made the mistake of saying I loved her. Now she believes we are engaged. Oh, perhaps it would have happened anyway. I'm not growing any younger and she is one of the most desirable daughters in the city: proper heritage, good money, high standing, beautiful in an American sort of way. And so, Mutti, it would appear you have your wish. I am affianced, after a fashion, but very unsure. I have come to question Seraphina's soundness of mind. I require your advice, as I have all my life. What should I do?

Rainer

7 June 1895

Dear Freddi,

My invitation to Juliette (as she prefers to be called) for "Robert le diable" began with disaster. Given that I have bided here more than eight months, I should have known not to reserve a place for her on the main floor, close to the stage. I had no idea the restrictions on seating someone of her color would extend to a personal guest of the maestro. I was beckoned from my dressing room before curtain to deal with a *disturbance* in the lobby: *A Negress claiming you supplied her ticket*. Ah.

In the lobby I argued with an insufferable usher, drawing a crowd and reducing Juliette nearly to tears. Seraphina's mother and father stopped to gape: I don't know which was worse—his goat-like grin of carnal curiosity or her pinch-faced moue at my supposed improprieties. I can only wonder if they will report the incident to Seraphina.

I was prepared to fire the idiotic little usher, but clearly Juliette did not want to sit where she was not welcome. She kept her composure and was shown to the last row of the first balcony. I was so unsettled the entire performance suffered.

Afterward, things improved somewhat. The hackman I had hired for the evening, a coal-black Caribbean piloting an elegant brougham, took it upon himself to protect Juliette as she exited. I was so grateful I tipped the man a week's wage and asked for several extra turns about Vieux Carré. Thus I had opportunity to speak with Juliette alone. She was very curious about the performance and asked far more penetrating questions than Seraphina—or her parents, for that matter—ever did. At one point she looked at me slyly with her feline eyes and asked, "Nuns dancing?"

She was referring to the ballet in Act III in which nuns rise from the grave and dance a bacchanal. I allowed it was scandalous.

"The nuns of my acquaintance. . . ," she said, "well, it's quite impossible."

"You are acquainted with nuns?"

Oh, yes, she was. She attended Sisters of the Holy Family Convent School for Girls. "Until I was fourteen," she said.

"What happened at fourteen?"

As soon as I said it, I heard how treacherous the question was. We had just drawn up outside El Paradiso on Basin Street and she said, "At fourteen, I was brought here. My father sold me."

I tried to say something or other—*How dreadful,* etc.—and she replied only, "I survived."

I sat frozen, causing her to ask the driver to help her down. I couldn't bear to part with her and I couldn't bear to go into the establishment. The player piano and laughter from inside carried even to the street and I refused to share her with a crowd. I asked for even more turns about the Vieux Carré. She and the driver both obliged.

Now, Freddi, you are asking me *What else did you do?* Forgive me, Brother, when I say *very little.* I was perhaps more timid than usual! I had *paid* for her, yet any advances—was I to ravish her as we turned off St. Peter's onto Bourbon?—felt inappropriate. She was so dignified. Not flirtatious like Seraphina and not importunate like Magda. Rather self-possessed, serene, unblenching. She spoke passionately of Isabelle, the heroine of the opera who redeems Robert with her love.

Driving through the warm night air, whispering together, watching her face pass through gaslight and shadow, hearing mockingbirds—always a good sign—put me in a foolish trance. But a man of my standing, hiding in carriages with colored courtesans and bickering with ushers in his own opera house? No no no.

The accepted and predicted course for me in New Orleans is to marry someone like Seraphina and fornicate as I please with someone like Juliette, feasting on my *gateau* and having it too, but it is all so... *bourgeois*. I crave beauty. Not only physical beauty, but beauty of spirit. Something higher. Don't laugh. If you are honest, Freddi, you want the same. Is it too much to ask?

Your tormented brother, R.

22 *August 1895*

Dear Mother and Frederick,

I am recalling today my earliest memory—that of seeing Frederick as a newborn in his bassinette. I was three and wholly unprepared for a squalling hobgoblin with a misshapen head to disrupt my only-child paradise. What a greedy little beggar you were, Freddi, wanting not only all of Mother's time, attention, warmth, and milk, but even some of Father's distracted glances as well. I was mad with jealousy, yet oddly fascinated. Your miniature fingernails, your transparent pate, your chubby thighs, and your all-consuming, ever-howling, toothless mouth. Suddenly the whole world loved Frederick best. And so did I—I adored you.

Why am I musing today on a thirty-year-old memory? Because I feel like a newborn and I crave, in my newness, that same adoration from you both—even from Father, if he reads this in the afterlife—the adoration bestowed on the new and the innocent.

Of course I am not innocent. For one thing I have lapsed in my correspondence, but, far worse, I have hoarded secrets and hidden my heart from you. Now I feel reborn because I am in love. And like Frederick as a babe, I am avid, hungry, starved, greedy for life. It feels a good kind of greed to want to live a complete life, a deeper life than I lived before, though it entails selfishness too—I want your approval and your love as surely as I did when I was a child. More so.

I imagine you have guessed by now the object of my affection is not Seraphina Carolina Kincaid Gerrity. Rather my beloved's name is Juliette Devereaux. Frederick has heard mention of her and been sworn to secrecy. Why? Because I am a coward and a fool.

Mother, Juliette is of mixed race, part African. Someday, if you wish, we will delineate for you the particulars of her heritage; but I beg you, let us not count droplets of blood from this or that side of the seas or this or that hemisphere of the earth. Living amidst the wild blend of blood, skin, and language that is New Orleans has cured me of my old preconceptions. To my shame, it was my own prejudice that led me to secrecy in the first place. What an ass I was, tiptoeing around ancient fears and hatreds like a patronizing prig.

Further, Juliette entered my life through the demimonde. I have asked her to leave that life, and perhaps she will, but I will love her regardless. She was sold at fourteen to a *maison de joie.* I can only imagine what she endured because she will not speak of it with me.

It is difficult to admit that I—conservatory-trained son of Austrian nobility, music- art- and gustatory-snob of New Orleans' Garden District, self-satisfied pursuer of high-strung gentrified young ladies—should receive lessons in humanity from a seventeen-year-old courtesan. But that is what happened. She has led me from the thirty-three-year drought of my existence into a world alive with delight, with new eyesight, with new reverence. Music sounds sweeter, wine tastes better, rain feels softer, and the very earth feels firmer. She was the most glamorous courtesan in New Orleans, with the world at her feet, yet she claims to love me. I only hope God grants me a long life that I might spend all of it adoring Juliette.

I saw Magda last week. She almost quit New Orleans because of Seraphina's harassment—showing up at the stage door, threatening her, insulting her. Once she tried to climb on the stage during Magda's performance in "Fédora." Seraphina's mother has taken her to Switzerland for a rest cure. Who knows? Perhaps you'll run into them at Klosters or Leukerbad. Meanwhile, Magda flourishes here, audiences worship her, and she's quite the bohemian—wearing knickerbockers and smoking cigars and seeing her name in all the gossip columns. She is affianced to a divorced actor who was excommunicated. That kind of *scandale* suits her perfectly.

And so, Mother, to the question of my own marital state. The race laws here are such that Juliette and I are not permitted to marry. We've consulted a priest and determined it is quite impossible. If only we could marry, the world would see what we mean to each other. I know when you meet her you will love her as I do. Frederick, I know you will love her too, and I am issuing my first warning: She is mine.

Your devoted, Rainer.

4

Straight Next Time

Without Christophe, we would have perished on 12 August 1901. That night a hurricane flattened buildings and flooded half of Grand Isle, Louisiana, but Christophe—eight years old and crippled—saved us. Guided us under the black-green skies and thrashing oaks, through the hell-roar of wind racketing our ears and the devil's own red clay grabbing our feet. In each lightning flare I saw Christophe leading my wife by the hand, shouting over his shoulder, *"Vite, Madame!"* Juliette clung to him, sliding on the slick path. Her hair streamed water and her satin shoes were caked with clay. I scrambled after them, falling, getting up, keeping close to the shredded, muddy hem of my wife's white dress. If I dropped back even a few yards, I feared I'd never see her again. With every breath I swallowed rain or choked on it. Christophe never faltered. He took us over the chênière and across the bayou to his mother's house.

Yes, I had thought about tropical storms before we came to Grand Isle. But anyone with the means to quit New Orleans in August—the heat, the cholera—did so. Grand Isle was merely the latest of my many attempts to cheer my wife. Vacations, rest cures, parties, journeys. Nothing worked. As an opera conductor, I had been invited to Atlanta, to New York City, and to Washington D.C. The more vibrant the city, the more listless was Juliette. The previous summer we had sailed from Boston to Naples on the SS *Ivernia* and continued by rail to Linz, where my mother took Juliette to Bad Ischl for a course of sulfur-bath treatments. From there to Paris and the Exposition Internationelle. We saw talking films, rode a moving sidewalk and toured the art exhibits in Girault's Petit Palais. One of the paintings, Cézanne's *Les Deux Enfants*, a tender scene of a little girl and boy playing with rabbits, upset Juliette terribly. How would we ever have a child if my wife could not even look at a painting of children?

The day we arrived on Grand Isle and took up our rooms at the Caminada Hotel, we looked from our window to the pearl-blue line of the Gulf horizon and Juliette said, "I feel her presence even here, Rainer. Do you feel it?"

She meant Thérèse, the daughter we had lost three years earlier, on 7 August 1898. The daughter who had never drawn breath in this world. From that day forward, Juliette had suffered a deepening melancholia that I feared was fathomless. She still embraced the notion that poor, unbaptized Thérèse was journeying through the ether and required rescue.

I kissed Juliette's hair and breathed her essence, eau de lavande and Le Désirable soap. "Darling, we must look to the future now."

"I know, Rainer. I'll try. I want a child as much as you do."

I kissed her neck, her forehead, her lips. When I touched the topmost button of her dress, she pulled away and went to the dressing table to study her face in the mirror and rearrange her cosmetics.

Of course, I had not endured the pain she had. When Thérèse tried to enter this world too early and died in the process, the ordeal nearly took Juliette's life as well. I flung myself into the task of restoring Juliette's health. Our cook prepared vast meals, only to have Juliette cry at the table and ignore the food. Her physician—the preeminent medical man in New Orleans—had said he was "reasonably certain" she could conceive again. But three years on, her body slender but healthy, she could not free herself of despair. At twenty-three, she was as beautiful as the day I met her. But I wanted children. And I wanted the lively, spirited wife I remembered returned to me.

* * *

While Juliette was rearranging her cosmetics a knock came at our door. I answered to find a tall, angular woman with dark eyes and sharp cheekbones, typical enough of the Acadians thereabouts.

"*Je suis ici pour Madame.*"

She was the lady's maid I had requested for Juliette. She wore a long peach-colored skirt, a white blouse, and a gold cross at her throat. She had a haughty tilt to her head and a copious amount of wavy brown hair swept back from her face with a band of white muslin.

"Do you speak English?" I asked. Juliette and I both spoke New Orleans French and could understand Acadian accents, but I did not like this woman's presumptuous attitude.

"*Pourquoi? Tu ne parle pas Français?*" She not only talked back but did so in the familiar.

"*Entrée*," Juliette called from the dressing table.

The woman paused and made the sign of the cross on the doorjamb. Then she brushed past me, opened Juliette's trunk without asking, and said, "*Bonjour, Madame. J'm'appelle Philomène.*"

I took my cigar case and left, while Philomène marveled at the first of Juliette's gowns to emerge from the trunk. Knowing Juliette, she would tip this bold woman far too much money and dispense gifts from her belongings as well. My wife never failed to empathize with servants.

While Juliette dressed, I spent a pleasant enough hour on the front gallery with my cigar and the day-old *Picayune* provided by the hotel. The "Weather Prophet" said a storm would cross south Florida but was expected to lose much of its force before reaching Louisiana.

When we went in for supper, it seemed the entire dining room—hum of voices, clatter of cutlery, flicker of candlelight—paused to regard Juliette at her loveliest as she made her way to our table. Whatever Philomène's faults, she proved an expert at enhancing Juliette's beauty, having dressed her hair in a swept-back style adorned with the jet-bead comb that had been my traveling gift. Juliette, too, was pleased with Philomène. "She speaks English perfectly well, you know."

"She could have told me as much."

"You insulted her by asking. These Acadians are very proud."

"She should remember who hired her."

The wine list had a Château Camensac Bordeaux, outrageously priced, but I ordered a bottle. When I offered my glass for a toast, Juliette added, "Philomène has a little boy. Christophe."

We dined on an excellent speckled trout marinated in mustard sauce. We watched the evening sky melt into pale coral and greenish blue as we strolled the white oyster-shell path that fronted the hotel. Creosote torches lit the way and discouraged most of the mosquitoes. The evening air was humid, but ambrosia compared to New Orleans. Juliette took my arm and I was feeling quite content until she said, "Philomène will bring me herbs tomorrow."

"You mean medicines?"

"No. Her own herbs. Apparently she's something of a healer."

"A servant. Who works at a hotel with wealthy patrons. And happens to have cures for sale?"

"She didn't ask for money."

"I'm sure she didn't. She knew with you she wouldn't have to."

"It can't harm anything. She's bringing her little boy too."

I coaxed Juliette onto the dance floor that night. The Caminada Hotel held an Acadian *fais do-do* every evening. During the first waltz she began weeping in my arms. Women and men alike glared at me, perhaps suspecting some cruelty on my part, perhaps unable to perceive that I love Juliette more than my own life.

Back in our suite, situated above the ballroom, we lay on the feather bed side by side, Juliette lost, no doubt, in a prayer for Thérèse, while the fiddles and accordions played on below.

*   *   *

Philomène brought the mysterious herbs—at least I saw a small linen bundle—when she arrived to help Juliette with the next morning's toilette. She also brought Christophe. I was shocked upon first seeing his deformity. The poor child's spine was twisted in some cruel way, causing the right side of his torso to curve in toward the left. He limped into our rooms behind his mother and gazed at us mildly through huge brown eyes. He had impossibly thick lashes and the same masses of dark brown hair as his mother. I could almost see Juliette's heart flood toward this unfortunate the moment he entered. She knelt beside him in her nightgown and said, "Are you Christophe?" Her fingers combed his thicket of hair off his forehead in a gesture I felt was reserved for me, though I had not experienced its pleasure in some time. "How old are you?"

"Eight years, *Madame*."

"And you are a help to your *Maman*?"

He nodded.

"Philomène," I interrupted. "What do you propose to do with Christophe while my wife is bathing and dressing?"

Philomène crossed her arms and looked from the boy to me. Just as I realized what would happen, Juliette said, "Rainer is going out for a walk. Christophe can accompany him."

Philomène added, "Oh, thank you, *Monsieur*. Very kind of you." So. English would be used if I cooperated.

I had envisioned a brisk tramp about the grounds and I'll admit to the unkind thought that Christophe would slow me down. I needn't have worried. His pace was determined. The contrast between his ruined body and his self-assurance was striking. He wore a loose muslin shirt and yellow cotton trousers that were hacked off and frayed an inch or two above his ankles. He galumphed along tirelessly, his bare, sun-browned feet slapping the ground at their bizarre angles. I wanted to walk toward the shore but Christophe said, "This way," and led me inland. At the end of the groomed path he plunged onward, on a rougher track that entered a thick copse of trees. We were soon under a virid canopy of oak, willow and dogwood, so dense the very air was green. "Christophe, where does this take us?"

He bent to touch a thick bush of long narrow leaves. "Citronella," he said. "For bellyache."

A few steps farther and he pointed to a branch of dogwood. I lowered it for him. Hidden among the leaves was a cluster of red berries. He plucked them out and slipped them into a pocket. "*Maman* keeps. For healing fevers."

I had another unkind thought, looking at Christophe's twisted spine and thinking *Maman* was not much good at healing.

Christophe caught me eyeing his deformity. He pressed his hand to his chest. "This come when *Maman* cure a cripple-man. Before I am born. His cripple go to me." He indicated another dogwood branch for me to lower. "*Maman* say I be straight next time. Next life." He picked more berries and pocketed them.

Christophe went on to identify countless plants growing on the chênière: okra blossom for boils, aloe for bee stings, calamus root for rheumatism, witch hazel, button bush, mustard, *la mauve*, sassafras, *l'herbe à malot*. We came into a clearing that muddied its way down to a bayou, where viscous green water mirrored mangroves on the other side. Suddenly shy with pride, he showed me his pirogue, tied to a broken-down jetty. He wanted to take me out in this tiny craft and looked crestfallen when I declined. His gaze went to some thin arcs of cloud, far off to the southeast "*Tempêtes*," he said. "Maybe twelve hours soon."

"Storm clouds?" I found this hard to believe. The wisps of vapor were as delicate as Alençon lace.

I asked him about storms. He had been born during the infamous hurricane of 1893. Given that the Caminada was the only hotel to have survived that storm, I had placed much confidence in its thick timber construction and a new seawall the hotel had boasted of in its advertisements.

"Christophe, what work does your papa do?"

"Papa he die. He be *pêcheur de chevrettes*."

That was the fanciful Acadian phrase for shrimper. "When did he die?"

"Same storm I am born."

I pictured Philomène alone in the storm, her crippled son coming into the world, her husband leaving it. I thought of my own deceased daughter, Thérèse. Groping for life, failing.

* * *

We returned to the hotel, expecting to find Juliette in the dining room. She was not among the guests lingering over café-au-lait and brioche. I wanted to go alone to our rooms, but Christophe trotted behind me like a puppy.

I opened our bedroom door to find Juliette in a chemise, lying on her back on the bed. Philomène sat next to her, bent over, with the side of her head resting across Juliette's abdomen, over her womb. She was muttering something, a prayer, I suppose, in French. Both had their eyes closed. The intimacy of their pose infuriated me. "Please tell me what is going on here."

Philomène stood up. Juliette struggled to prop herself on her elbows. "Rainer, I am sorry. If you would leave us for a while."

"To do what?"

"I'll see you at luncheon. Please leave us."

"No. This woman is not a doctor."

"*C'est une cérémonie. Tout simplement.*"

"Damn it, woman, speak English." There were not going to be any ceremonies, simple or otherwise, in our room at the Caminada Hotel where we came to rest, not to be bullied into back-country mumbo-jumbo.

Christophe ignored my outburst and climbed onto the bed. He knelt there in the rumpled linen and took Juliette's hand, pressing it to his smooth boy's jaw. "*Madame* is sick?"

Juliette smiled at him. "Don't worry, Christophe."

"*Maman* helps you. *Maman* helps many folks."

"Philomène," I said. "Remove your son from my bed. I am asking you both to leave."

"First I will prepare a tea for *Madame*."

I was not accustomed to being contradicted by servants. But Juliette looked at me with such pleading. She knew very well I never refused that look.

"If you must," I said. "I'm going bathing." I went to the wardrobe for my bathing things and was further infuriated when Philomène produced them from a drawer instead.

"I am with you," Christophe said, getting his twisted body off the bed. He even took my hand as we passed the stained glass windowpanes on the stairway landing.

The hotel had a contraption, a cart pulled by mules along a railroad track, to take guests to the bathing beach. The silly thing was filling now with rambunctious children and their large-hatted mothers, and I was in no mood to join them. I set off at a stride. Christophe, of course, claimed to know the best spot for bathing, so again I found myself following him. His beach was indeed lovely, completely deserted, but without the customary cabins for changing one's clothes. There was nothing for it but to strip down with Christophe gazing at me from beneath those lashes. "Run along," I said. "Don't you surf-bathe?"

He made a face. "For city folks," he said, but he wandered down and waded partway in, clothes and all.

The Gulf water, keen with scents of salt and seaweed, enfolded me, warm and buoyant, its turquoise clarity shot through with sunrays and suspended bits of sea life that had—for all I knew—traveled the world to arrive there that morning. I stroked hard into the low swells. For a time I forgot about Juliette and Philomène and the useless cures. When I came out, I found Christophe in the most peculiar posture. He sat in the shallow water, little waves lapping about his waist, his eyes closed in concentration. Then he struggled to his feet and studied the horizon. "Something coming."

I found it difficult to be concerned. Under the pale blue bowl of sky, Grand Isle seemed a paradise. True, the breeze was up, but that was a relief after New Orleans.

* * *

When I finally did meet Juliette in the dining room, luncheon was almost over and we sat in the big room alone. Juliette looked lovely in her delicate white dress, the dress that would be ruined in the storm. White lace was arrayed at her creamy brown throat and her white satin slippers peeked out from the hem of her skirt. She appeared energized, with a light in her dark eyes that I had almost forgotten. I should have been grateful, but I did not wish to credit the source of this alteration.

"Are you going to tell me what was going on up there? Do you even know?"

"She was merely praying for my strength. Many physicians lay on hands, you know that."

"She is not a physician."

"I thought you wanted children."

"I thought we both did."

"Will you take my word that I feel better today? Is that not progress?"

I could not deny she looked well, which had been my deepest wish for months. Now I saw it, I was angry. Juliette was happily eating her entire plateful of shrimp boulettes, even sopping the sauce with her bread like a farmer in from the fields. I gazed at her with admiration and confusion, wishing simultaneously to scold her and make love to her.

We ordered coffee after lunch. While Juliette put an alarming four cubes of sugar in her cup, she looked at me and said, "Philomène has asked me to visit her, at her home."

I suddenly noticed how hot the dining room was. Why had we ordered coffee in this heat? No one on this damn island knew how to make decent coffee anyway. "Juliette," I said, "I cannot permit that."

"Why not?"

"Let's go outside. It's too hot."

Juliette did not press the subject of visiting Philomène. She agreed to sit with me on the greensward next to the hotel where guests played croquet or had lemonade and ginger cookies brought out. I took the *Picayune*, but the breeze was suddenly much stronger, making it difficult to read the newspaper. A few other guests were about. A little boy and girl were knocking croquet balls to and fro. The girl grew bored and wandered over and regarded us, curious, her little laced shoes planted on the grass and her little-girl stomach thrust out. She was a beautiful child and, I realized, about the age Thérèse would have been. Juliette tried to smile, but I saw tears fill her eyes instead. The girl fled and buried her face in her mother's skirts.

Juliette pressed her fingertips to her eyes. I feared if people saw her weeping again, as she did on the dance floor, they might come after me with pitch and feathers. "Dearest," I said, "would you prefer going back inside?" She lowered her hands and shook her head.

I looked past Juliette, down the oyster-shell track, and saw the unmistakable form of Christophe limping toward us. "Look," I said, "here is Christophe. He will cheer you."

His breath rasping, his dark hair wild in the wind, Christophe said, "*Maman* say come to our house."

"Tell your mother no thank you," I said.

"Storm coming. Safer at our house."

"Safer than the hotel?" I asked.

"Safer at our house," he said again.

"Rainer," Juliette said, "please, I'd like to go."

"It won't be a bad storm," I said. "The hotel is safe."

Christophe grabbed Juliette's hand. "*Allons, Madame.*"

Like a jealous lover, I removed Christophe's hand. "Go along home to your mother, Christophe. *Madame* and I are fine."

* * *

The evening's *fais do-do* was to proceed as usual, although by sunset the wind was roaring about the hotel and treetops were thrashing its roof. After Juliette's bout of weeping the previous night, we had no plans to attend the dance. But we did sit in the front room of the hotel with glasses of cognac. We stayed well back from the windows but could see trees tossing against the twilight sky. Juliette barely spoke to me. As she swirled cognac round and round in her glass, I feared she was again dwelling on the memory of Thérèse.

The storm built with breathtaking speed. Darkness fell and then, in a disconcerting turnabout, the skies lightened again as mountains of liquid-silver clouds sped in from the southeast. The first raindrops hit the front windows like bullets hurled one by one from the bulked gray sky. That changed all at once to what seemed like barrels of water, one after another, being splashed against the building. The first lightning strike was much closer than I anticipated, illumining the hotel grounds not like daylight, but something much starker. In the second burst of lightning, we saw the phantasmal form of Christophe struggling across the sand-grass in the downpour. The manager tried to stop the dripping child from entering the lobby, so Juliette set down her glass and ran to meet him. "Christophe, why have you not gone home?"

His thick hair clung to his forehead and streamed water into his eyes. He blinked furiously, his lashes flinging droplets. "*Madame*, you must come. You must."

The first windows to shatter were the stained glass panels on the landing. The wind created pressure changes—I felt them in my ears—that gave the sensation the roof might lift off. Some of the guests fled the ballroom for their cabins or for higher ground. Another group cowered at the back of the ballroom. Twelve of those would perish later that night when the second floor—our bedroom—came down on top of them. I never learned the fate of the family with the little girl we saw on the greensward.

Juliette allowed Christophe to pull her out, into the driving rain. Amid the pandemonium of hotel guests running this way and that, I had no choice but to follow my wife and the boy. We took the route across the chênière that Christophe and I had walked that morning. How different it all was now, in the dark, with shorn branches flying from trees and sheets of rain drowning the air.

Christophe never let go of Juliette. It took all my strength merely to keep up. A willow was down across the path. Before I could lift Juliette over it, Christophe pulled her over the roots, half dragging her by the armpits, not hesitating for a moment. The pirogue, which I had deemed too dangerous that morning in the clear light of day, became our only hope for crossing the rain-pelted black bayou. Christophe poled the little craft unerringly, dredging impossible strength from his crooked limbs. Juliette sat on the center plank of the pirogue, eyes closed, face lifted to the rain and lightning.

* * *

At last we did arrive amid the howling wind at Philomène's house, a stout wooden cabin on brick risers, sheltered in a grove of very old red oak. Those massive trees, I imagined, had shielded the place from many a gale. Philomène leaned against the door as we entered, then shouldered it closed again. Suddenly all was dry and still, and we were met with the tangled aroma of hundreds of medicinal plants. The ceiling was hung with swags of drying herbs, row after row, like an inverted forest of bunched sticks, leaves, flowers, and roots. Most were unknown to me. I recognized chamomile and the citronella leaves Christophe had shown me that afternoon. Swags of garlic and red pepper hung over a cook stove where a pot simmered. On the wall around the cook stove hung two tin washtubs, two dried raccoon skins with striped tails dangling, numerous skillets, pots, pans, and baskets. Filling another wall was a glass-fronted cabinet of small, corked bottles and, next to that, a makeshift altar covered with a white, fringed cloth. Among the many candles flickering there, I made out statues of the Virgin and St. Francis, several crucifixes and rosaries, a Bible, a scattering of what I believe were sharks' teeth, a dried skin of a water moccasin at least five feet long, a small portrait of an old woman, and a pencil drawing of St. Roch, the plague healer of medieval France. Tiny blue glass cups held crumblings of dried herbs.

The moment we entered, Philomène made Christophe strip off his wet clothing. This he did after one quick glance at Juliette, who was already moving toward the altar, drawn by the candle-light and icons.

I had one glimpse of Christophe's poor back, corkscrewed about itself, before Philomène wrapped him in a rough blanket. She ladled some of the steaming concoction from the stove into an enamel cup for him. He sat at a wooden table on one of the fat oak boles that served as chairs. An old milky-eyed setter, who had greeted us at the door and wagged her tale limply when she recognized Christophe, curled up behind him.

Philomène and Juliette stood with their hands folded on the altar. I wanted Juliette to remove her drenched clothing but did not dare speak now. The wind was a steady roar, like a locomotive that never stopped passing. The house had no glass windows, merely open-air ones, covered now with thick wooden shutters. Water leaked in and darkened the warped sills.

Juliette and Philomène prayed aloud, murmuring in counter-point to the drumming of the rain. I sat across from Christophe. He pushed his enamel cup toward me and I drank the remains of his tea. It was bitter, but I'll admit it revived me. I looked at Ju-liette's thin back in the sodden white dress and suddenly thought of my daughter in her little white coffin.

Christophe, hunched there in his gray blanket, watched me. The enormity of his accomplishment now settled upon me. I stretched my hand toward him and he took it. His fingers were still wrinkled with damp but already warming and pulsing with his Acadian blood. To think I had tried to bar my heart against this boy. I rose and stepped to his side and clasped him to me where he sat. He was all twisted, trembling bones but unbowed, in his way.

Perhaps, in my heart, I was clasping Thérèse, whose spirit I had abandoned in my striving to restore Juliette. Perhaps my daughter waited for my attention even now, like that little girl on the greensward. I pulled Christophe closer. Feeble though it sounded, I said *merci*. He nodded against my ribcage. That small movement pulled some trigger that released a sound from my throat that shocked me. Thankfully, the storm noise almost drowned it, but Juliette did glance at me before returning to her prayers.

I wept, clutching Christophe. It was agony to picture Thérèse. She took on the form of the little girl playing croquet on the greensward, but it was Thérèse, I am certain. If I had the power, I told her, I would grant her safe passage, such as we had received from Christophe.

*   *   *

Our second daughter, Catharine—the one destined to survive—would struggle into this life nine months from that day, on 12 May 1902, as wild from the moment of her birth as the tumult that night on the chênière. Catharine—we called her Cate—was the child who would inherit my green eyes along with the duskier hues of Juliette's mother's skin; who would be at odds with the world even whilst in the womb, and completely ungovernable once out of it; who would reject every refinement and luxury we could offer her—French tutors, dance cotillions, piano lessons, art classes—in favor of running wild through the Vieux Carré and teasing boys on street corners and slipping into dives on Perdido Street to hear old Negresses sing "Black Snake" and going to cockfights, palm readers, voodoo priestesses and Canal Street astrologers; who would run away from Sisters of the Holy Family convent school at age fifteen and turn up six months later in a saloon in Slaughter, Louisiana, singing those same Perdido Street blues shouts, wearing a shiny cobalt dress and already pregnant by the piano player. Oh, her son Louis was a joy, but he barely dampened her never-ending desire to consume whatever she could of this world.

What My Last Man Did

Sometimes, when Cate was a small child, the confident tilt of her head, with its thick black curls, would remind me of Christophe as I saw him that night, poling his pirogue in the storm. His silhouette against the wet green sky did not look deformed. He seemed the one perfectly formed being in the storm.

* * *

A crack of thunder violent enough to wrench open the earth drew us from our reveries. I released Christophe. The dog whined and resettled. Juliette crossed herself. Philomène turned to the stove and ladled another cup from the pot.

While Juliette sipped the tea and stroked Christophe's head, Philomène bustled about, eventually taking from a cupboard another blanket and some threadbare towels. These she handed to me. She pointed to a ladder leading to a kind of loft. "Christophe's," she said.

Juliette looked at Christophe, who was almost asleep where he sat. "*Mon petit*, may we take your room?"

He looked up, his eyelids heavy. "*Oui, Madame.*"

Juliette, her dress still trailing drops of water, grasped the sides of the ladder.

I followed my wife up the steps.

5

What My Last Man Did

Cate wriggles into the blue beaded dress. LaFitte's kitchen reeks of boiled mullet, old cabbage, burnt onions. The cook Josiah hacks pork ribs and tells his boy to feed the stove. The blue beaded dress is a gift from Huston—God knows where he found it. Robin's-egg *soie de chine* with cobalt beads clicking all down its length. "Blue for blues singing." That's what Huston said when he gave her the package, nervous, like a boy in a brothel. She hasn't told him yet she's pregnant. She's almost sure. The mullet makes her want to heave. But no doctor in Slaughter is going to check a fifteen-year-old colored runaway for pregnant, so she'll have to wait and find a midwife.

A cockroach crawls across the calendar—July 1917—woodblock of a Shreveport & Texas locomotive gushing steam. Out front, in the saloon, the band warms up. Only Huston on piano is any good. The drummer, Franklin, hopped up on Raleigh Rye, keeps rushing the beat. The bass man, Alphonse, harbors the notion he can improvise.

The saddest Cate can feel is to conjure up her father. He must wonder where the hell she is. She balls up all that sadness in her stomach, going through the kitchen to the saloon and out to the upright piano. Small applause. Huston beams to see her in the dress. She keeps the sadness in her stomach with the baby and starts "Chain Gang Blues."

If only she could sing it like LuLu. When LuLu sang "Chain Gang Blues" it wasn't so much a singer singing a song as it was the naked soul of a girl carving up her heart for a roomful of strangers. LuLu taught her the moans, curving slurs, bent blue notes. "Like a willow drooping." Everything else has to come from your gut. Most girls singing blues grew up poor. Cate figures nobody would listen if they saw her parents' house on St. Charles Avenue in New Orleans. Near the end of "Chain Gang Blues" she notices Duval is here again. Even in the gaslight she can see his parted hair and Sunday suit.

*　*　*

Wilson Duval, broiling in his best twill, tilts his chair against the wall and watches Cate. She has a new blue dress that looks like a gift from Satan. At twenty-five, Duval—the youngest-ever sheriff of East Feliciana Parish, Louisiana—knows his mission: return Slaughter to the righteous. Some thought he was a joke until he cleaned up The Haze, where all the hoboes lived. Raided the place in April with his idiot deputy. Hauled in offenders, including Cate.

First time Duval ever saw her. They thought she was a boy until the deputy knocked off her cap and all this hair spilled out.

Pawnee Bill's Wild West Show rolled into Slaughter that same day. As if the action in The Haze weren't enough for one lawman in a single day, Pawnee Bill's vast canvas tent burst into flames at sundown, funnel of sparks twisting heavenward and red reflecting off the clouds. From half a mile away, Duval could smell the burning flesh and hear the horses tethered up inside. Pawnee Bill himself proved a hero, pulling women—white women, colored women—from the flames, going back time after time until he didn't come out.

* * *

I stole Cate's dress off a high-nose white lady at the station. Stole her trunk and fenced the jewelry and a coat and alligator shoes. But the jiggly beads and shiny blue are Cate. Not just for the way she sings. Blue I'll bet you anything is the color of her soul. I never knew a girl so happy and so sad at once. Smiling, crying, yelling, loving, eating, singing. She's a runaway train no matter what.

Take my word, I won't be in Slaughter forever. Chicago. That's where the hot music and the smart niggers are. Me, I'm Chickasaw by blood, Huston by name. But it's niggers took me in and Uncle Midas taught me how to play. Chicago's where we'll make the real money, make Cate famous. Me as manager. Bookings. Contracts. The business side. I'm not good enough on piano, I know that. I'm just honky-tonk.

* * *

Cate hated Sister Magdalene, her silent glide down corridors, her halitosis and her fleshy nose, her sagging chin pinched in a wimple stiff with starch. On Cate's first day at Sisters of the Holy Family, Sister Magdalene rooted through her suitcase and threw away a bottle of *Nuit de France* perfume, an ivory silk chemise and a pamphlet of love poems in French, which Sister Magdalene called filth. In the next bunk was LuLu. They joined in hatred of Sister Magdalene, hatred of five AM Mass, hatred of their parents who sent them there. Leaning over cornmeal mush and biscuits, LuLu talked about her fellow, Benedicte. Cate talked of where the walls were lowest and what time the abbess went to bed.

* * *

Of the four saloons in Slaughter, Cate picked LaFitte's when she heard the piano from the street. Even in bright day, he played like midnight in New Orleans. Dark. Drenched. Sad and hopeful both, like setting out, like LuLu and the rails.

Cate walked in quickly, before cowardice could stop her. Sawdust floor, smell of bad tobacco, bluebottles sifting heavy air. "You need a girl to sing." She didn't say it like a question. The drummer Franklin laughed so loud Josiah peered in from the kitchen. Cate gripped her hands behind her, let her eyes plead her case with the copper-colored piano player, his strange high cheekbones. Her audition consisted of twelve bars of "South Train Blues," repeated twice, and the piano player Huston nodded solemnly each time.

* * *

Duval can't pry his eyes from Cate—a slithering blue flame up there in her shiny dress. She drops her voice to a growl for the line that says *You can't do what my last man did*. Inside Wilson Duval's Sunday suit, his apparatus strains against the twill.

He wants to know what the hell's a Chickasaw from Oklahoma Territory doing in his parish anyway? And who ever heard of one of them playing piano like a colored? And why did this Huston stand and watch that night while the tent burned down?

When they raided The Haze and hauled Cate in, she had on a man's flannel shirt of dove gray and a waist-bunched pair of dockworker pants. She excited Duval more profoundly than his wife ever had in proper skirts—or out of them. Cate looked like she might spit when he asked her where her people were. What he meant was "How much Negro blood?" and she knew it. With those oval eyes, she could be a princess from a South Sea isle. He let her go when the alarm bell clanged—the tent ablaze at Pawnee Bill's.

Three days later she was with the 'breed. Huston.

* * *

From the start, she felt safe with Huston. They have a room on Cypress Street. Huston's five years older and he's been around. He kisses like he's been to every world inside her. For a week he slept in clothes and kept a sheet between them. Asked if she'd ever done it. Now they do it every night and day, and Cate's afraid she'll get too happy for the blues. She's never planned one day into her future. Now she has a baby coming and a man to love.

Huston acts the boss around the boys but with her he's empty, scared. Wants to know how a little girl can sing so big. LuLu taught her. The twelve-bar blues, the rhymes, the chords. And why is she in Slaughter? LuLu's fellow Benedicte got them out of Holy Family on the freights. They ended up in Baton Rouge, LuLu singing in a barrelhouse. They were safe there for a while. One night a man came in and asked for "Catharine." Within the hour Cate was in disguise and on a freight. Got off in Slaughter, in The Haze.

* * *

Duval remembers every moment of that first time he saw Cate. She said she was twenty, from Knoxville, surname Paradiso. All lies, Duval is certain. She is sixteen at most. He knows New Orleans talk and a fake name when he hears them. Still he wanted to kiss her sunburned mouth. When the idiot deputy knocked her cap off, he got three scarlet scratches down his cheek for the favor. She smelled like a hobo's cook-fire, which was maybe why her voice makes Duval think of smoke. Smoke and twilight and that time of day a man should feel good about going home.

* * *

Cate could lie forever in the narrow bed with Huston. He's the only one she's told about her family. How her father used to bring his opera singers home to teach her voice. His singers all adored him. Maestro Rainer Schofeld of the New Orleans French Opera Orchestra.

Her mother? Her mother, the hypocrite, owned the Basin Street bagnio called El Paradiso and always wanted Cate to be on stage. Well, now she is. Her mother, the hypocrite, the too-beautiful octoroon, pretended no part of Africa could reside within her veins. Or her daughter's veins. All the Ursulines, priests, French teachers, dressmakers, tutors, cotillions, governesses, and European husbands in the world cannot deny the legacy of blood. On the street they didn't treat Cate white, so why pretend? The night she snuck into a barrelhouse on Perdido Street and heard a girl sing "Black Alfalfa's Jailhouse Shouting Blues," she decided the way off the slave ship was to get back on.

For her sins she was sent to Holy Family. Now she has the family she wants. LuLu—somewhere—Huston, the unborn baby, the band.

* * *

Two AM. Duval sips cold tea at his table in the back. LaFitte's steams with every shade of sweaty skin—black, brown, yellow—copper if you count the 'breed. Amber honey if you look at Cate. No white women of course, but two white monte throwers from St. Helena Parish who keep a loud game going in the corner. On the other side of Slaughter, he'd have to bust it up.

He recognizes Daphne, the nigger girl who irons for his wife. She has given Cate an ostrich plume and fixed it in her hair. Cate starts "Bleeding Heart Blues" and Daphne dances by herself—or writhes like a heathen in a cheap cotton dress. A big buck gets up to grab her by the waist and grind against her. Cate groans the line,

Not a soul to ease your mind. Duval's soul has not been easy since the night he questioned Cate. Sacrilegious dreams. Putting a gold ring on her finger. She wears an ivory satin gown. He carries her into a yellow clapboard house where rosewood banisters curve toward shadows and heaven.

Up on the stage, Huston stamps the beat with one foot while his fingers flick across the keys. Where does that 'breed get his money? Lafitte pays him a dollar a night and a few folks throw nickels. Yet Huston's always buying rounds or sporting a vulgar silver watch-chain on his vulgar white vest. He plays piano with those insinuating fingers, a nasty brown cigarette stuck in his slit of a mouth. No doubt those fingers have explored every inch of Cate. No doubt she's cradled his thick Chickasaw head and let his slit of a mouth slobber on her breasts.

* * *

I'll take a piss before we start "Evil Man Blues." There's a spot out back where all the men shoot it to the petunias. Funny how the stars looked the same in Oklahoma. Yes, I set the fire. That bastard Duval calls me 'breed but all my blood is Chickasaw. We didn't belong in Oklahoma. They removed us. You ever been removed? Men like Pawnee Bill—an Irishman from Pittsburgh, the bastard—take Chickasaw and pay them pennies to demean themselves. They pretend to be Comanche. You ever seen Comanche and Chickasaw side by side? I set the fire. I didn't know the canvas would go up that fast. Next day, Cate comes to LaFitte's and tells us she can sing. Jesus Christ can she sing. I would not have done it if I knew her first. Loved her first. A girl like Cate, you treat her different. Yes, I set the fire. Doesn't mean I don't love Cate.

* * *

Daphne's proud Cate sits beside her for the break. The boy brings Cate her Coca-Cola with fresh-chipped ice. Daphne opens her Chinese paper fan.

What My Last Man Did

"You are built for that dress, child." She touches the blue beads, adjusts the ostrich plume. "Are you gonna do 'Black Snake?'"

"Shit, it's hot." Cate holds her hair up off her neck.

Duval, out of nowhere, out of shadows in the back, pulls up a chair and sits like he's invited. "Ladies."

Cate lets her hair drop. Daphne says, "Why Sheriff, how's your wife?"

"I need to talk to the Indian," he tells Cate.

Daphne intervenes. "Then talk to him."

Cate stares into her drink. "He's out back."

"That's too bad. I'll have to talk to you."

* * *

Duval has never dared to take the dream beyond the rosewood banisters. He carries Cate forever up and up the curving flight of stairs.

He's ashamed he's struck his wife. She nags him like a banshee. Why does he go to LaFitte's? Why must he carry a pistol off hours? Why can't she join Ladies' Aid? Why did the tent catch fire? Why can't she wear earrings to church?

He prays to God that he might love his wife again. He prays to God to guide his hand in being fair and helping folks. Didn't he assess a white man cheating coloreds out of indigo? Didn't he disarm the crazy mulatto by the tracks who swung a pitchfork and screamed of Armageddon? Isn't he fulfilling every aspect of his oath of office?

* * *

Daphne hears the whole room hush because Duval sits down with girls. This sheriff will do anything. He beat that poor mulatto to a bloody mess beside the tracks. A simpleton who went to Lamb of Our Redeemer Baptist. The old men in The Haze weren't hurting anyone. Duval just makes a show of helping coloreds. His wife's a frightened rabbit in their fancy house. But he better watch out with Daphne. She'll backtalk God if she gets mad enough. For some reason Duval says to Cate, "I know police in New Orleans." Cate sips her Coca-Cola, sweat-shine on her upper lip.

Daphne says, "Yeah, I know the King of Chicago, but what of it?"

"You think anyone in New Orleans would want to know about this fellow Huston?"

Even Daphne knows to shut up now.

"You think anyone in New Orleans would want to know about Cate 'Parra–dee–zo'?"

* * *

The baby's name will be Louis Paradiso. He will have the copper skin of Huston, Cate's abundant black hair, her father Rainer's Austrian green eyes. He will be so beautiful even Cate will concede she sees her mother there. He will be born January 30, 1918 in Charity Hospital on Tulane Avenue in New Orleans and return with his mother to her parents' mansion on St. Charles Avenue. Cate will inherit her parents' fortune, invest it in a recording company, lose it in '29. She will take her life at thirty, leaving Louis on his own.

* * *

Daphne kicks Cate's foot beneath the table. Get away. Cate sets down her Coca-Cola and tries to stand. Duval stays her with one hand. He seems a middling white man, but he won arm wrestling and target practice both at Parish Fair. Some folks gasp to see him clamp her amber arm.

Huston strolls in from the kitchen. He reads the room. He feels the thickness of the room and sees Duval and Cate. He doesn't change his walk. He comes through the thickness of the room like nothing's different.

* * *

What My Last Man Did

"Huston," my mother said, "stay with me." Then I watched her die. In a hell-on-earth called Sulfur, Oklahoma, when I was four years old I watched my mother die from liquor—curl up in a ball, white foam bubbling from her lips. We didn't belong in Oklahoma. She rolled into a ball at my feet on the dirt floor, her stomach blown up like a pig bladder full of water. I curled up with her, shit all over, she was naked, but I curled up with her, dead for a day, maybe two. The stench is with me still. The only thing good from Oklahoma was the Negro woman, Mrs. Lovett, took me in. And her brother, Uncle Midas. She had six black children of her own, and still she took me in.

*   *   *

Daphne's heard all the versions. Some folks said the bass man Alphonse put the dirk in Huston's hand. Others said he had it in his shoe and Alphonse merely pulled Cate to the side. No one knew Duval inside his fancy suit would have a pistol. Even when he took it out, no one thought he'd shoot. He was smiling. He smiled at Huston and his little shiny knife.

Cate said, "Stop it," but it came out like a whisper. Daphne put herself in front of Cate.

Duval was smiling. "This is for the tent and not the girl," he said. Whatever that meant. Daphne never knew.

Two explosions. So loud Daphne thought Armageddon was upon them, like the simpleton said.

Two holes in Huston, one in the arm—it would have healed—and another right above the silver chain. As he stood there, puzzled, a crater of blood opened on his white vest. He took a table and five whiskey glasses with him when he fell. From his knees, he looked at Cate. She went to him. Helped him stretch out as if to sleep. No one spoke. No doctor in Slaughter would come to LaFitte's for a copper-colored man. Duval ordered everyone out. They all stared at him. He pocketed the gun and left.

Huston took till dawn to die. His eyes rolled up and his feet scrabbled in the sawdust. Josiah packed the wound with a poultice of honey, garlic and cayenne. The bleeding would not stop. You could smell it when his bowels gave way. Cate stayed with him on the floor, knees crushing the cobalt beads into his blood.

* * *

Wilson Duval, the youngest-ever sheriff of East Feliciana Parish, Louisiana, walks down the hard-packed clay of Main. The monte throwers, if he needs them, can testify the 'breed waved a knife. A 'breed who by the way belonged in Oklahoma.

Chuff of locomotive and the crossing whistle ride the breeze from north of town. Must be the freight out of Baton Rouge, the three AM.

* * *

In the room on Cypress Street, in the narrow bed that smells like Huston and his smokes, Cate watches dawn creep through the curtains. She grips her stomach where she thinks the child might be. How can she feel so empty and so full? Empty like the azure sky she saw once over Slaughter, with one tiny cloud to show its emptiness. One tiny baby to show her loneliness.

Will it grow? Will it grow no matter what? If she cries aloud for Huston, will it grow? If she damns Duval to hell, will it grow? If she lights out on a freight for St. Charles Avenue, New Orleans, will the baby live? Cate will crawl there over coals if it means the child will live. She will kiss her father's hands, his feet, and bear her mother's wrath. If need be, she will die so that Huston's child will live.

6

Tchoupitoulas

I. St. Michael and the Heavenly Host Hospital

The first time I saw Louis, his fingernails were rimmed in the dried black blood of his dead mother. He lay flat on a bare hospital bed in his underdrawers, looking small for fourteen. His gaze was fixed on a light bulb glaring from a green metal shade overhead. The cage of his ribs stretched his dark brown skin taut with each breath. He didn't look at me or at Emile.

A doctor arrived. Silver hair, gold fountain pen. His first question was, "What do you know of the boy's heritage?" Typical white medical man in New Orleans in 1932, more concerned with race than with doctoring.

"His mother was one-sixteenth," Emile said. The word *Negro* was implied. One-sixteenth *Negro*.

The gold pen scratched a note. The doctor looked doubtful. One-sixteenth wasn't as dark as Louis.

Emile added, "His father was a Chickasaw Indian. Pure bred, I believe."

Another note. "And the mother died this morning? A suicide?"

"Yes."

"The mother was your client?"

"Yes."

"And the father is dead?"

"Yes."

Shot by a sheriff in East Feliciana Parish. Years ago. I was relieved Emile did not mention it now. With that burnt-copper skin and those high-planed cheekbones and near Chinaman eyes, Louis would have enough problems. He looked not quite Negro, not quite Caribbean, possibly Indian, possibly Mexican, possibly *Eskimo* for all the speculation he was likely to get.

Emile and I are one-eighth. The way it works in New Orleans now, two light-skinned *gens-de-couleurs* such as ourselves, with a darker child. . . . Well, it turns heads, but it's better than the other way around.

"Will you be supplying funds for the boy's hospital stay?"

Supplying funds. Why don't you look at your patient, you bigoted son of a bitch?

Emile presented his card: *Emile St. Victoire, Attorney at Law.* Perhaps the ornate script was enough to bespeak *funds.*

"The boy is severely traumatized." The doctor still spoke only to Emile. As the wife, I might as well not have been there. "We'll keep him for two days."

A sister in a white habit bustled in with an armful of linen and a white enamel bedpan. The doctor moved down the ward. Emile tried to pull me away too, but I turned back and covered Louis's hand with mine. He looked at me then, terrified and questioning.

"Louis. We'll be back for you."

His eyes shone glassy in the flat light. He gripped my thumb.

"We're your new mother and father. I'm Genevieve."

He gripped harder, his palm hot and damp. The nurse rolled him onto his hip and smoothed a sheet under him. My husband said, "We should go." Louis released his grip and closed his eyes.

Then we were outside, pushing onto a crowded streetcar that made a slow climb up Esplanade through the stifling evening air. It was Friday and all the shops were closing. The sun drooped in the west like a ripe apricot behind a maze of garden magnolias.

Emile was silent as far as Bayou St. John. Then he said, "The boy will need a bed," and took off his trilby to wipe his brow.

The boy will need a bed. As if I hadn't thought of that. As if the things Louis would need weren't adding up inside my brain. Clothes. A room. Love. What did he eat? What size was he? What school grade? What religion? Probably godless, given that mother of his. Cate Paradiso. The so-called jazz singer everybody admired so much, who as far as I could tell had squandered her life, utterly squandered it. Emile told me how for years she hauled Louis up and down the eastern seaboard with her ragtag musicians in second-class train cars and second-hand Studebakers, singing in clubs, the great *chanteuse*. She made a success of a recording company for two or three years, but it all went bad after '29. She had to come back to poor little New Orleans and take up in the big house her parents left her and run it into the ground, or so I had heard. Louis probably had two years total in a proper school and now he was fourteen and his mother dead by her own hand.

At home over supper as I poured iced tea Emile said, "I'm sorry, Genevieve. It was a foolish promise."

I hope you didn't miss that: an apology from Emile. "Is it even legally binding?" I asked. Emile had promised Cate Paradiso he would be Louis's guardian if anything happened to her.

"Yes. It's legal. I signed it. I didn't see this coming."

Later, Emile turned on *The Collier Hour* from WNOC while I washed up. I didn't want to talk. I had to think.

I was fifty-two. Emile was fifty-nine and we had been married for thirty-four years. Our biggest disappointment had been our inability to have children. Not for lack of trying. In the early years, we went at each other like feral cats in an alley, like rabbits in a cage, as if our God-given task was to populate the earth. But no child was conceived.

Still we had a good life. Emile had his law practice. I volunteered at Sisters of Mercy, where they took in poor women. I tried my hand at watercolors, found I was good at it, and even taught classes. I played canasta and mahjongg with a group of ladies who were well-meaning, if a little silly. What I wanted was to travel—there were always excursions advertised: Florida Keys, Cuba, Jamaica. Except for a childhood trip to Lafayette—how I remember the excitement of setting out—I had never left New Orleans. But over the years Emile turned inward. He worked himself near to death and he scrimped money and he thought travel was foolish. Once hard times hit, I was grateful he had saved so much. But I had wanted more. More life. More adventure.

II. *The House on St. Charles Avenue*

If Greek gods ever settle in New Orleans, they will settle on St. Charles Avenue, under the canopy of live oak, amid the scents of jessamine and pomegranate. All that greenery absorbed sound too, as if people here could afford silence as well as mansions.

The house was like a white ship plying a green ocean, its double-deck gallery reaching up through the trees and the second-story windows topped with Arabian curves. But the front steps creaked as if to herald the ruin and decline inside Cate Paradiso's home.

The front-room carpet had been taken up and I smelled moldering wood. The floorboards looked dirty around the edges and lighter under the piano. Emile had told me about the piano, a gigantic black Mathushek grand worth two thousand dollars. It would be sold to pay debts.

"Hello?" I expected to find the estate agent Emile had hired to sell the place and its contents. What contents remained. Cate Paradiso had been selling things for cash. The faded ochre wallpaper showed dark rectangles where paintings had once hung.

"Hello?" I started up the stairs, carrying the suitcase I brought for Louis's things.

In a room off the landing a man was leaning over a small desk, opening a drawer. The desk held a world globe; the rest of the room had a single bed, a small chiffonier, and, on the wall, a mechanical drawing of a steam locomotive with all the parts labeled. I expected the estate agent would be a white man but this man was Africa-black. A Northern Negro—or so I suspected from the close cut of his suit and the pomaded height of his hair. I said, "I am Mrs. Emile St. Victoire."

He looked amused. "If you say so." Everything about him was large: large elongated head, large barrel chest, large square teeth, large hooded eyes. Perhaps forty years old.

"Are you the estate agent?" I asked.

"No." He closed the drawer. "Raphael Mercier. Folks call me Rafe."

"I've come for Louis Paradiso's things," I said.

"Me too." He put his hand on the desk as if to stake this claim.

I brushed past him to the chiffonier and opened it. A few shirts and a wool jacket drooped from hangers over a jumble of clothing underneath. "I'm to be his mother," I said.

"His mother?" Mr. Mercier opened the desk drawer again and started pulling out what looked like folded maps.

"Yes. My husband and I are Louis's legal guardians." I knelt and opened the suitcase. I picked a boy's cotton shirt from the pile of clothes. The collar was a gray crescent of grime.

"But Louis knows me from way back," Mr. Mercier said. "I told him he could stay with me."

I folded the shirt into the suitcase. "Well, he can't, Mr. Mercier."

"It's Rafe," he said.

"Rafe. Should I know who you are?"

"I'm one of Cate's sidemen," he said, as if all God's creation knew this.

"Sidemen?" I took the wool jacket off its hanger.

"One of her musicians."

"I see." The jacket was good quality but the lining was torn.

"Trumpet." Rafe pointed to himself and waited for the significance of *trumpet* to reach me.

"I see." I smoothed the jacket into the suitcase.

"You never did hear Cate sing?"

"No, I was never so blessed." I pulled socks from the clothing heap and tried to make pairs. Nothing matched.

"You don't care for jazz music?"

"No." I didn't know anything about jazz music, but I was growing angry with the dead Cate Paradiso. Her son's clothes were a mess. I gave up and rolled a brown and a black sock together. "And I don't care for mothers who abandon their children."

"Oh, don't be judging on Cate," he said. "Please."

"I do judge her." I held up the sock ball. "Why did she do this?"

"I don't know, ma'am. She was broke, I know that." He looked about the room. "But she was far and above all this."

"All what?" I demanded. "Above caring for a child? Earning a living?"

"Maybe."

I watched his face, his sad eyes, and I wondered if he had been in love with her.

"She was born to sing," he added, "I'm sure of that." He tidied the maps into piles on the desk.

"Mr. Mercier," I said.

"Rafe."

"Rafe. I see you've lost someone who meant a lot to you."

He blinked slowly and I was afraid he might weep. Instead he put his long fingers on the globe and began to twirl it slowly. "It's funny," he said. "Cate was like . . . like the sun. You know?"

I wanted to say yes, but I had never known anyone like the sun.

"She had a way of holding the center." Now he gave the globe a furious spin. Pink and amber continents blurred by, aquamarine oceans.

"The center?" I asked.

"On stage," he said. "When we played." He watched the spinning globe slow down. "She was all light. She had these huge, wide eyes and she would signal all the cues to us, like she was the center and we would all get there together."

"Get where?"

He laughed lightly. "Heaven?"

For some reason that embarrassed me. I gave up on folding and busied myself scooping clothes into the case and snapping it shut.

"You seen Louis?" Rafe asked.

"He's in St. Michael's." I lifted the case by its handle, as if I had a train to catch.

"He all right?"

"He's severely traumatized, Mr. Mercier. Rafe."

"I know. I'm the one who found them."

"Found them where?" I asked.

Rafe pointed to the floor below. "By the piano," he said. "Cate cut her arms." He drew a finger from wrist to elbow. Again on the other side. "Louis was trying to close the cuts with his own hands."

I thought of the dried blood under Louis's fingernails. Rafe went on. "The cops came." He slammed the drawer he had been emptying and straightened to his full height. "They took me for questioning. Me." Now his eyes did film with tears. "Who loved her."

"I'm sorry." I started for the stairs but Rafe blocked my way.

"Will you at least bring Louis to her funeral?" He reached for the suitcase. I let him take it. I hadn't even considered the funeral. "All the musicians want to play for her. A parade and all." He carried the suitcase downstairs and outside to the streetcar stop.

III. St. Roch Cemetery

Louis ran ahead of me when he caught sight of a squat man snake-wrapped inside a tarnished brass tuba. They tried to hug each other but settled for some secret musicians' handshake. Other horn-players and drummers and their wives or girlfriends also grabbed Louis's hand or embraced him, praising Cate and wiping tears from their eyes.

About thirty of us gathered under the lacebark elms on Rampart near Ursulines and started the slow walk north and east through the side streets toward St. Roch Cemetery. A chestnut mare pulled a creaking wooden catafalque that held Cate's white casket. Louis plodded along beside it, eyes cast down. I felt helpless to comfort him. Rafe—in a white tuxedo with a yellow satin sash across his chest—led the parade. His trumpet flashed gold in the sun but his feet tramped the route with grim resolve.

I had known Louis all of three days. I was madly in love with him. I loved his calm voice and wide, smooth forehead. I loved the oval curve of his skull through his cropped black hair and the oval mystery of his eyes as he watched my every move. He had a way of softening his gaze and tilting his head when he looked at me. For my part, some instinct—some need for something I couldn't figure out—made me copy that look and return it. This mirror image gaze that we exchanged several times a day somehow drew us close together.

When Emile first brought him home from the hospital, Louis was wearing the knickerbockers and knee socks and white shirt I had sent along. The clothes were too small on him and he looked ridiculous. But he had such dignity. Imagine you are fourteen, in a new house with new people—a grumpy old lawyer who tells you to sit down and eat and his flustered wife who gives you some silly aspic and beet salad—and your beloved mother is freshly dead and your pants are too tight in the crotch.

All that, and Louis held his own. He was polite, deferential, nearly silent with lovely manners. So I had to credit Cate Paradiso with something. He knew to say please and thank you and sir and ma'am. If I drained my tea glass, he jumped up and brought me the pitcher, his clear ivory thumbnail pressed along the rim.

After supper I showed him his room. Yes, we had procured a bed and outfitted the back room where I used to have my art things. He studied the white eyelet dresser scarf and, above it, my own watercolor of a paddle-wheel steamer and asked, "Is this where I live now?"

I realized no one had told him anything. I sat him down on the blue chenille bedspread. "Louis, before your mother died, she asked Emile to always take care of you. If anything happened to her."

"Why did she do that? Because you have money?"

"Well, we don't have so much money," I said.

"Because I know a lot of folks."

"Yes, I know." I wanted to appear the firm parent, but I was nervous. I was scared he might run away to Rafe or to anyone familiar.

"My mother knew all kinds of folks," he said, as if he hoped we might forward him on like a piece of mail.

* * *

The funeral band—trombones, saxophones, two tubas, a cornet, snare drums, and Rafe's trumpet—opened with a mournful

"Nearer, My God, To Thee." By the time we reached Elysian Fields the parade had drawn a hundred people or more. It would seem everyone in the Quarter knew Cate Paradiso.

Walking alongside the catafalque, I felt old and dull in my navy dress and brown shoes. Most of the girls and even a few women my age wore bright frocks and many had feathers in their hair, which I learned was a trademark of Cate's. Again, I felt Louis watching me and, I suppose, reading my unease, because he took my hand. I almost wept with gratitude. In the year I would have him, he would do this often: sense what I needed and try to help.

The band did "Lonesome Road." Rafe played a solo on "Lead Me, Savior" that was so beautiful it took me back to church as a young girl, where the notion of God was entangled with my own longing for a grand destiny. Little did I ever dream I'd be walking hand-in-hand in my middle age with a strange and beautiful boy who could explain funeral music: "That's shoutin' blues," he'd say about a certain number, or "Roosevelt Sykes wrote that."

* * *

The second evening at our house—the scene much the same, except I skipped the aspic and I had taken Louis to Wainwright's for proper clothes—I saw Rafe through the window, coming up our walk with Louis's globe under one arm and a guitar case under the other. When Rafe stepped inside, Louis ran so hard into his arms that the globe clattered to the floor.

Emile stood up and said, "You must be Mr. Mercier." Rafe reached around Louis to extend his hand, but Emile wouldn't take it. "I'll thank you to stay away from the boy," he said, even as Louis clung to Rafe.

"What?" Rafe almost smiled in disbelief, splaying one of his big hands across Louis's back.

"I'll ask you to leave my home." Emile could be powerful in court, but at that moment he looked weak next to the towering Rafe with his hooded glare of scorn.

Rafe chose to ignore Emile. He let Louis tug the guitar case from his hand and they sat on the carpet and opened it like eager youngsters readying a game. The guitar case held no guitar; it held the maps and the locomotive diagram from Louis's room on St. Charles Avenue. It held a Hohner harmonica in a cobalt blue box. Apparently Rafe had been teaching Louis to play the harmonica.

I sat near them on a footstool, drawn by their excitement. Louis undid the accordion folds of a *Gulf Oil Motoring Map of the East Coast*. I glimpsed the red-artery roads tying Virginia to Pennsylvania, New York to Massachusetts, with connecting nodes of big cities and small dots of towns along the way, places Louis had most likely been that I would never see. Even the knowing way he handled the map—he pointed to Atlantic City and laughed with Rafe at some private joke—made me ache with envy for all the living he had already done without me. He traced his finger up to New York City. "I used to live there," he told me proudly. "I'll take you sometime."

"I always wanted to see it," I said.

My husband would live two more years before his heart attack, and I don't think he ever forgave me for that moment.

* * *

At the gravesite in St. Roch Cemetery, someone read the twenty-third Psalm while Rafe blew a plaintive wail in the background, so soft it was like the very air was keening. Then a young girl led a blind man out in front of the crowd. He had a tin guitar slung over his shoulder and a green glass bottleneck on the little finger of his left hand. "Willie Johnson," Louis whispered.

The man half-hummed, half-moaned his way through a lament while he slid the bottleneck across the guitar frets and picked out sad twangs and heartbreak chords. He rocked from side to side while he played and his eyelids fluttered over empty white sockets. "'Dark Was the Night,'" Louis added.

The crowd turned so quiet. It seemed the whole city had come to a halt. A few of the ladies got to their knees, then Louis did, and so, gradually, almost everyone else did. I wasn't sure I could get on my knees, but Louis steadied me and I made it, with only one crack loud enough to be embarrassing. We stayed there several minutes after the song ended. I had slipped into prayer, asking God to give Louis a chance in this world, and when I opened my eyes, Louis was still beside me with bowed head and tears on his cheeks. People rose one by one and many walked past Louis and touched his shoulder. "She's singing with angels," someone told him. Or, "She loved you, son."

When the procession left St. Roch, the band struck up the joyful songs and fast marches. They played an up-tempo "We Shall Walk through the Streets," which they had played as a dirge on the way in. I knew this was tradition, but the bright tunes felt wrong, given that Cate Paradiso had left this world too early.

The musicians gave it their all—trombone slides flashing skyward and the tuba players chuffing along with sweat stains spreading on their backs—but the sadness was too deep. One by one, people got tired, gave up, and hugged Louis one last time before breaking away from the procession. Louis drew Willie Johnson over and introduced me as his "Auntie Genevieve." I don't remember even speaking to the man, so thrilled was I by this new name Louis bestowed upon me and would use forever after. He only ever called Emile *sir*.

Rafe and a few others stopped in one bar and then another along St. Claude. Louis and I waited outside, fanning our faces with funeral cards. "Do you think she was beautiful?" he asked, holding up his mother's picture on the card.

There was no denying the voluptuous curve of her mouth or the haunted cast of her eyes. I took Louis by the shoulders. "Yes, Louis, she was beautiful." I pulled him close. My first real embrace of my *son*. His hands were warm on my back and he let me crush him against my chest for a long time.

Rafe got drunk. Louis saw me to the streetcar and then went back to make sure Rafe got home. Emile was furious when I came home without Louis. "He'll take off with that black bastard and we'll never see him again," he said, pacing the living room. An hour later, Louis returned and went silently to bed.

IV. Tchoupitoulas Railway Station

It's all damp ochre brick that soaks up cinders and weeps out sooty streaks down the cracked façade. Tchoupitoulas. The station where Louis hopped a freight. The engineer they call King—big man from Mississippi with a red-bulb nose—finally admitted as much to me when he saw me on the platform bawling. "Aw, ma'am, half the boys in Louisiana are riding rail. He'll be back."

Maybe.

When he left, Louis took with him the final pieces of dream I had propping up my life. Suddenly I saw the paltriness of the years I had strung together. Except for that wondrous year with Louis, my life seemed to consist of putting pork chops on the table for Emile or turning out too-precious watercolors or riding streetcars to no place in particular. Yet I didn't blame Louis for leaving.

In the months following the funeral, Rafe came over all the time —as long as Emile wasn't home. He would drink iced tea with me in the dining room and talk about Cate, sometimes breaking down in tears, which he used as an excuse to sip from a flask. He would sit with Louis in our back yard for harmonica lessons after school. That is, if Louis was in school, which on most days I doubted. More likely he was train-watching and hauling coal for pennies and running wild with the boys who hung around Tchoupitoulas Station.

*   *   *

The first postcard came two months after he left. Postmarked Chattanooga, October 1, 1933, addressed to me in pencil. The entire message: *Louis Paradiso.* As if first and last name were required for me to know he was alive.

I lied to Emile about Rafe. Or at least I hid the facts. It was easy to see that Rafe was the father Louis needed, but Rafe was drinking and it was getting worse. I begged him to stop and he would go on the wagon for a few days before I smelled it on him again. He would shake his head and grin the grin that must've captivated Cate. "I'm sorry, Auntie G., I'm no good," he'd say.

It all caught up to us when Emile saw the first reports from Hayward Academy, where he had insisted Louis matriculate. Poor grades and strings of absences. You'll call me a sad excuse for a mother, but I didn't care. I didn't care because I saw by then how the world did not reveal itself to Louis in traditional ways, not in scholarly ways, not through math or Latin. For Louis the world was maps, music, timetables, trains.

* * *

The second postcard arrived two months after the first and was loquacious by comparison: *Chicago Brrr Some work in yards. Stinks but pays good. Louis Paradiso.*

* * *

To keep Rafe away, Emile stepped in with a Restriction of Contact from a judge and police to back it up. It scared Rafe enough that I never saw him again. It even seemed to scare Louis for a while so that he tried to stick with school and homework. For the next term, I sat with him most evenings over social studies lessons and algebra problems, both of us tired and bored. Too bad every class wasn't geography. We kept the globe on his desk and sometimes he'd simply gaze at it while I tried to solve for x.

One morning at four-thirty I was up making coffee because I couldn't sleep. The house was quiet and dark, when suddenly I heard a key in the front door and in walked Louis. He had been sneaking out to hear Rafe play in the Quarter.

What My Last Man Did

"He's my friend," he explained.

"I know, Louis, but I can't have you out alone at night."

"Why not?" He wasn't arguing. He really wanted to know. "I've been out a lot at night. And Rafe needs me."

"Rafe has to work life out for himself," I said, feeling cruel. "Let's leave him be for a while."

A few weeks later we followed Rafe's funeral procession—less than a year after Cate's—as his body was taken to St. Roch to rest near hers. I wonder if grief runs one death behind. Louis's grief over Rafe seemed like delayed grief for his mother. For weeks, I heard him crying in his room or watched him lug his satchel home from school in a fog of misery. One day I caught him burying something in the back yard. It was his harmonica.

And so when I found the slip of paper under my coffee cup— *Bye Auntie G.*—I didn't blame him. I cried, but I didn't blame him. He'd been fighting the whole summer with Emile over going back to school. Wordlessly I showed the note to Emile, who stared at it for a long time and then said, "Let him see what it's like out there. He'll be back."

* * *

The third postcard was from New York City. By then it was springtime, 1934, and he'd been gone for a year and a half. The picture on the card was of The Cotton Club. *Man here remembers Cate. Have work. Louis Paradiso.*

* * *

The farther Louis receded from me, the greater my love grew. I loved his courage, how he listened to his inside voice, how he corrected his course. I'd get angry for a while—*How could you?* and all that—and then go back to loving him.

I copied some of his courage and started traveling on my own. I remember the first time I went up to the window at Tchoupitoulas Station and asked for a ticket for Vicksburg. Four hours up the line for most folks, but for me, a journey into a new world. Or into myself. I felt like a character from the funny papers, bending back bars to get out of jail.

Louis would not return for four years. I had kept the house after Emile died and still lived there with a girl who helped me. I think I knew from the knock on the door that it was Louis, rangy and shy, just turned nineteen. "Auntie Genevieve," he said in that same soft voice, those same Chinaman eyes crinkling up in that same innocent smile. "How are you?" As if he'd been gone a few days.

He towered over me as we embraced and I cried, maybe harder than I had cried when Emile passed. As if to cheer me up, Louis said, "I have a girlfriend." He brought her by and I tried to like her but she seemed cheap and frivolous. Louis spent too much money on her.

I took longer and longer trips. I've been to Memphis, St. Louis, and—for one glorious week—Chicago, where I listened to jazz music, the only lady of a certain age in white gloves sitting in a 39th Street club.

What I love most is setting out. The first open sweep of river with cloud shadows moving on the pale brown water. Is that what Louis saw? Mules in traces in the cane fields, cotton waiting to be picked, or the fresh bales under burlap on the loaders. Pain, glory, vistas. Ladies in traveling suits and men with valises. Kitchen gardens spooling past with peas strung up and cabbages gone to seed. Shacks, barges, factories. Barefoot boys running by the train, waving, hollering. All the parish seats: East Feliciana, South Vacherie, Pointe Coupee, Iberville. Sometimes I have one of Louis's maps with me, opened on my lap, and I trace the route as we roll along.

7

Do Nothing Till You Hear From Me

Louis melds from the yellow afternoon into the tavern's soft dark. Blinded, he goes by smell—spent matches, oiled wood, stale beer. But a tunnel of sun from a back door reaches the bar. Eggs glow white as light bulbs in a jar of brine. The slim silhouette in the mirror—angled cap, straight shoulders, khaki uniform—turns out to be Louis's own reflection. Hands in pockets, he touches a fold of bills, a crumpled letter, and his good luck charm.

A tall Negro barman looms behind the taps, watching. The place serves colored. Two GIs perch on barstools next to a girl in a black feather hat. Louis nods a greeting. The men are probably from McClellan, but he doesn't know them. Someone else, another girl, sits alone in the back. Louis pays for a beer and takes it to a booth.

It's easier, going to colored places. He is tired of explaining that he is only one-thirty-second Negro; that one grandmother was an octoroon, but his father's side was all Chickasaw. He is tired of explaining, too, that he did not see action in Europe or the Pacific. He did not kill Japs, he did not kill Jerries, he did not storm beaches. He spent VJ day—two months ago—making forty-two vanilla cakes with chocolate icing in the officers' mess at McClellan Airfield. Not a fit job for a man of twenty-seven—patting sprinkles into icing—but the army saw his copper-colored skin and made him a cook. Since his discharge he's managed to get ten miles from the base, to Sacramento.

He lights a Pall Mall and pulls the crumpled letter from his pocket. His lucky charm—a carved pelican, three inches tall, with knowing eyes—comes out with it and he sets it on the table. He smoothes the paper, which is dated September 23, 1945, at the top and signed *Love, Lily* at the bottom. In between, every sentence Lily wrote contradicts itself. *I think about us and our love, but Mama says I'm young for nineteen and don't know love from influenza.* And, *My best dream is to fly from here and we get married in a little church, but Mama says it is self-centered and stingy to leave your kin.* But Louis has sent money for the train anyway. Maybe Lily will make it from New Orleans to Sacramento and join him. It's the only thing holding him here. She's the only thing he's wanted for the past three years' worth of mashed potato vats; flats of white bread in cellophane bags; triplicate forms for truckloads of ketchup, pickles, ersatz mayo, and Spam; a stupid white apron and cap; swaggering pilots who called him "boy"; and, in his off-hours, never-ending games of poker and dice that absorbed all the rage he and his messmates would never dispel in combat.

He reads the letter again, though he has it memorized. He recites his promises to himself. He will hold onto what money he has—three hundred in discharge pay and $12.90 from his last game on base. He gets this one beer, but he will not rent a room, he will not eat in a café until Lily arrives. Then he will take her in his arms, run his palms over her skinny hips, feel her breath in his ear, and get them a room in the best hotel that will take a copper-skinned man with a buzz cut and a light-skinned Louisiana black girl.

Suddenly, behind the letter, she is standing there. Or at least for a moment he thinks so. But it is not Lily. It is the girl who was sitting in the shadows at the back of the tavern. Japanese, as far as he can tell, though he has nothing to go by but wartime cartoons of kamikaze pilots and the emperor. He has never met a Japanese girl. Her dark hair is something like Lily's, curled back from her face.

"You're not colored," she says.

"Neither are you."

She is a small woman, but hugely pregnant. So pregnant that Louis feels something like shame. As if some unmentionable craving is on display. The baby tents out the front of her blue-gray dress, decorated with a white collar and big buttons down the front. She squeezes herself onto the seat across from him, swiveling her legs in last. She wears white ankle socks with brown and white saddle shoes.

"I'm Nisei," she says. "Do you know what that is?"

He nods.

She lifts his cigarette from the ashtray. "Well, what is it?"

"Japanese kid." He shrugs. "I mean, Japanese . . . lady."

"Second generation Japanese-American." She puffs once on the cigarette, coughs, puts it back.

"I'm Chickasaw," Louis says. "You know what that is?"

"Indian kid?"

"On my dad's side, anyway." Louis tries smiling at her, but her eyes are hard and her mouth is grim.

She looks at his stripes. "I see you are an Indian *sergeant*. Kill any Japs?"

"I spent the war in California," he says.

"Kill any Japs?"

Louis clears his throat and drinks down half the beer. "I ran the officers' mess at McClellan. That's the kitchens and dining rooms."

"I know what a mess is," she says. "That's what they called it at Manzanar." She cuts him a look, daring him to make something of that.

He hasn't thought much about Japanese internment camps and he doesn't want to. "Can I buy you a beer?" he asks.

"No."

"Cigarette?" He offers the pack.

She shakes her head. "In case you hadn't noticed, I'm soon to have a blessed event."

Louis nods and tries to keep his eyes from drifting to the front of her dress where her breasts push out the nubby, blue-gray cloth. "What's your name?" he asks.

"Mrs. Ruth Tanaka." She offers her hand. "You can call me Ruth."

"Louis Paradiso." It's strange to shake hands with a girl. Her fingers are damp and warm, almost boneless.

"You sound like you are from the South," she says.

"New Orleans."

She touches one of the buttons near her throat. "San Francisco."

The girl from the bar gets up and goes to the jukebox. When she drops her nickel in, the jukebox lights up red and gold. Duke Ellington. "Do Nothin' Till You Hear From Me."

"Once when I was little," Louis says, "I met Duke Ellington."

Why did he say that? He never talks about those days. Or his mother. Or nights like that night they met Ellington. Winter, 1927. Sleet on the windshield of the cab. Harlem neon streaky in the dark. Louis was nine. He called his mother by her first name—Cate—and he thought all kids went to the Cotton Club. Cate's recording company, Wildcat Records, had put her briefly in the big time. That night they heard Duke Ellington's orchestra and met the man himself backstage. White suit, white tie, white suede shoes. He talked to Cate in a low voice. Leaning in. Filling her glass from a slim bottle. Bending down to shake hands with Louis. Later Louis woke up on the scratchy red couch, alone in the room with Ellington's rehearsal piano. Sheet music and ashtrays all over the place. Louis settled on the piano bench and played "Chopsticks" six times. He smoked the last cigarette from a glass box shaped like a swan. He read the lyrics on the music: "tonight—I—shall—sleep—with—a—smile—on—my—face." Five hours later Cate came back and took him to a café for breakfast.

"So you're a big shot because you met Duke Ellington?" Ruth asks.

"Didn't mean that." He crushes out his cigarette. "It's just my mother. She was something."

"Is she in New Orleans?"

"She died when I was fourteen. And my old man died before I was even born."

"My husband died in Italy." Ruth touches her gold wedding band. Her finger is puffed up and the ring looks tight. "In Livorno."

"Sorry to hear that." Louis lights another Pall Mall.

"He was with the 442nd Regimental Combat Team."

Everyone knows about the 442nd, the Japanese-American regiment. Most were recruited straight from internment. Many were decorated. "Those were brave guys," Louis says.

"He didn't even have to go. He could have stayed in Manzanar." She picks up Louis's pelican charm and rubs her finger over its black eyes. "All you had to do was not sign their loyalty oath and the army wouldn't take you."

"He probably wanted to fight," Louis says. "I wanted to fight."

"Heroes." Ruth shrugs. "Get your guts shot out and your family gets a flag."

"I'm just saying, I can understand why he went. But I'm sorry he passed. I'm sorry the baby won't have its father."

"Oh, Sergeant, count on your fingers and figure it out. Livorno was '43. He's not the father."

Louis fumbles his cigarette from the ashtray and takes a deep drag.

She holds up the little pelican. "What's this?"

"Old charm from my grandmother. Louisiana people think pelicans bring luck."

"You needed luck in a kitchen? What? Not to burn your fingers?"

"I'm no coward." He takes the pelican from her hand.

"I didn't say you were."

The letter from Lily is still on the table. Ruth looks at it. "Love letter?"

"Not exactly."

When she picks it up he says, "It's personal."

Ruth starts reading, and Louis sits back. Let her read it, he thinks. He could use some advice. He watches Ruth's eyes trail over Lily's handwriting. "This is one mixed-up girl," she says.

"What do you mean?"

Ruth squeezes her eyes shut and straightens her back, touches her hand to her spine and shifts her weight.

"What's wrong?" Louis asks.

"With me? Nothing." She hands him the letter. "With Lily here, you're in trouble. She's never going to leave her mama." Ruth swings her legs out of the booth and pushes herself up, knuckles white on the edge of the table.

Louis stuffs the letter in his pocket. "Where are you going?"

She gives him a withering look and plods toward the back hallway. Louis wonders if she might deliver the baby right there in the ladies'. It looks that close.

He finishes his beer. Hell, she's probably right. Lily's not coming. She's too far away, he's too broke, and the few times they made love before he was drafted cannot compete with the dragged-out dead-time of war. Their picnics and walks cannot compete, nor the hot picture-show house where they held hands, nor the time they saw the traveling preacher in Metairie heal a cripple; not even the time—that day of china blue sky and cool air—when she laid the old chenille bedspread on a patch of junegrass and unpacked cold fried chicken and a pecan pie. They had walked halfway to West End from the end of the tramline, and her white sandals got muddy. How she worried on those shoes, trying to clean them with fresh leaves, trying to pretend she was occupied with something other than him and what he had in mind, more urgent now that Pearl Harbor had cast its shadow. He remembers Lily covering her mouth whenever she laughed, which was often, to hide her crooked teeth. He marveled at how clean and shiny her fingernails were. Something about those fingernails and the white sandals and the pecan pie and the way she smelled of Cashmere Bouquet and the way she had picked the most hidden spot in a grove of chinaberry told Louis that was the day she would finally let him. Let him unbutton the back of the polka-dot dress and slide it off her creamy brown shoulders and let him roll on top of her—a moment he would replay so many times in his mind's eye at McClellan that it became a kind of prayer or religion or fixed thing, like a tunnel that led to his future.

He had spent the war wanting her, but she wasn't coming. Like every guy at McClellan, he spoke of girls in short bursts of lewd remarks, but dreamed of girls in serious dreams about post-war bliss, postwar jobs, postwar houses and babies, home-cooked meals and Chevrolets and lawnmowers and Saturday night dances and baseball games and beers and paychecks and snug neighborhoods with fences and trees and mailboxes. Lily wasn't coming. He buys another beer for himself and a Coca-Cola for Ruth. He asks the two GIs at the bar where a man might find a poker game. One of them nods toward the back hallway. "Card room right here," he says. "Come back tonight. Around eleven."

When Ruth returns she looks from the Coca-Cola bottle to Louis and sits down.

"Listen," he says. "Why don't you let me buy you dinner?"

"Sergeant Paradiso, I have done nothing but insult you since I sat down."

"Call me Louis."

She laughs. Her teeth are a little bit crooked, like Lily's. She covers them with her tiny fingers, the way Lily does.

"I have a different idea," Ruth says. "I will make dinner for us."

*   *   *

She has a place a few blocks away, over the Woolworth's. Metal stairs up the side of the building. One room with a little sink, stove and icebox lined up at one end and a narrow iron bedstead with a thin mattress at the other. A shaky-looking table with one chair on the bare wooden floor. A window overlooks the street. The shade is pulled partway down, casting the whole place in an orange cardboard light. He sits in the chair and she opens a cupboard. He sees a can of Vienna sausages and a can of Folgers coffee.

"Ruth, you don't got to do this."

"Just hold on. I have fresh eggs, believe it or not. You want a fried egg?" She grips the curved edge of the porcelain sink as if it's the only thing holding her up.

"I'm a cook, remember? Let me do it." He gets up and holds the chair for her. She lowers herself carefully onto it.

"Do you have a place?" she asks.

"No." He opens the icebox and takes out the egg carton. Two eggs inside.

"How was this Lily supposed to find you? Not that she's coming."

"Santa Rosa Hotel. Man there said we could leave messages. Get mail too."

"Where do you sleep?"

"Someplace cheaper than the Santa Rosa Hotel." He doesn't want to tell her he has slept on park benches and washed up in gas station restrooms. He finds a can of lard and a cast iron fry pan and gets the eggs started. "You saving those sausages for royalty or anything?"

"Help yourself," she says.

"You got an onion?"

"Do I look like I have an onion?"

He opens the sausages and adds them to the pan.

"Hideo could cook too," she says. "My husband."

"What did he do? Before?"

"Hideo? He was an engineer. He worked for a company that built things. Big things. Bridges, tunnels."

"Man, that's good work," Louis says.

She has one plate and one bowl, so he divides the food between the two. She has one spoon and one fork, and she insists he take the fork.

"Aren't you going home to San Francisco?" he asks. He stands with his hip against the sink to eat.

"No." She pushes a piece of egg white onto the spoon with her finger. "San Francisco is not large enough for me and this baby and my mother and my father."

"Why not?"

"I have disgraced them." She holds the bowl up. "I cannot eat these." He takes the sausages out with his fingers and puts them on his plate. "As long as I was the widow of Hideo, the golden warrior from the glorious 442nd, I was a shining light. After I made a baby with a dirty *gaijin*—a camp MP, by the way—the shining light went out."

"Guy-jeen?"

"Foreigner."

He stabs the last of the sausages. "Did he—uh—"

"Force me?" She tries to stand with her bowl, but he motions for her to sit down. "He did not. My mother said to pretend like he did, but I could not."

Louis puts the dishes in the sink. "Doesn't he want the baby?"

"He doesn't know about it." Ruth goes to the bed and sits down and pries each shoe off with the toes of the other foot. "Why haven't you returned to New Orleans?"

"Because I'm sick of that place. You can't be anybody but the guy people think they know. If you try, well, then you're showing off."

"Would you rub my foot please?" She sticks out one foot in its white sock.

He crosses to the bed. "What do I do?" he asks. But before she can answer he kneels and takes her foot in his long, brown hands and kneads it the way he did pastry dough back at the base.

"You're good at that," Ruth says. "So what show-offy things did you want to do?"

"I don't know. Something. A college or something."

"You have ambition."

"Tell that to Lily's mama." He takes her other foot and starts in. "Partly it's California. Feels like you can do anything here."

Suddenly he wants to run his hand along her calf. Maybe along her thigh. He wants to feel closer to her. As if he could show Lily he has options and he doesn't care if she doesn't come. He lets his hand linger above her white sock. She looks down at him

"Don't get any ideas," she says.

His neck grows hot and he gently lets go of her foot. "I wasn't," he says.

The room is quiet except for cars passing on the street. "Do you need money?" he asks. "I have some."

She lies back on the bed and stares at the ceiling. "You must keep your money for your girlfriend."

"I thought she wasn't coming."

"She's not. But you can hope."

*　*　*

At night, the jukebox is louder. Couples dance in front of it, swaying to Dick Haymes crooning "You'll Never Know." The song weaves through a din of talk and laughter. Every barstool is taken and every booth is full. The same barman is rooted to the same spot behind the taps. The floor is sticky with beer and the air is dense with smoke.

Louis shoulders his way to the back hall and finds the card room. A single bulb lights an oval table where six men play five-card stud. He hangs back, hands in pockets, fingering his money and the lucky pelican. One of the card players is the GI he spoke to that afternoon. Two others are also in uniform, and one of these is a private who looks about seventeen years old. The other three are old-timers—black men with creased faces and pomaded hair. One of them cashes out and the others invite Louis to sit down. When the seventeen-year-old shuffles the deck, the sound works on Louis like a drug. His lungs expand. His chest feels light. Every card dealt him is a welcome, forbidden gift, like a pin-up girl stepping out of the wall, saying *Touch me*. He loses five dollars in the first two hands.

"Didn't you leave today with that nip?" It's the GI from the bar.

"She's a Nisei," Louis says.

He snorts. "What's that, a kind of nip prostitute?"

Before Louis left Ruth's room, he washed and dried the pan and their few dishes. Ruth fell asleep. Louis covered her with the limp blanket from the foot of the bed. The room was already too warm, but he wanted to do something for her. "She's a nice lady," he says.

The GI shakes his head. "If you say so."

On the third hand, when Louis lifts the corner of his hole card and sees the king of hearts, his mind slips completely into that altered state where he is both anchored to the earth's core and flying, with stars and moons rushing by. All he can see are the cards down a kind of tunnel. Time slows down. Sounds drop away. Money floats. Cards fall. On that hand he makes the five dollars back, kings over eights. But by two AM he is down one hundred dollars. The seventeen-year-old is the big winner, raking in pots while flicking a toothpick between his thin lips and never changing his expression.

At four AM Louis is down two hundred and wondering what happened. He stays in for another hour, winning and losing the same fifteen dollars before leaving the tavern with ninety-six dollars in his pocket. He starts walking toward the Santa Rosa Hotel. Daylight is coming, a cave of yellow opening in the east. Starlings land on telephone wires and set up a racket. He feels hollowed out, the way he always does after a game, win or lose. Suddenly he remembers what the GI said about Ruth. Nip. Prostitute. He should have gut-punched the guy.

The Santa Rosa doesn't have a real lobby. More like a narrow, dusty living room, with a scarred front desk and a broken-down sofa next to a dead palm tree in a pot. A boy behind the desk scans the comics in the *Sacramento Bee*.

"Any mail for Louis Paradiso?"

The boy takes eight or ten envelopes from under the desk and slaps them down. Louis flips through them. Nothing for him. Nothing from Lily. "Thanks." He hands them back. The boy looks up. "Oh. Paradiso? Somebody here looking for you."

"A girl?"

"Yeah. She's—" he looks at a register—"She's in room eight."

What My Last Man Did

The stairs are creaky and smell like old Pine-Sol. Louis takes the steps three at a time and knocks on eight.

"Who is it?" Lily's voice, close to the door.

"Baby, it's me. I'm here."

The chain scrapes and she opens the door. She looks thinner than he remembers, standing there in her bare feet and belted blue cotton dress with the little flower print. Her curly hair is mashed flat on one side. Her eyes are swollen and spilling tears alongside her nose. "What's wrong?" Louis asks.

She stands with her arms limp and presses her face against his chest. Her hair and clothes smell like the train, like soot and crushed-out cigarettes. He closes the door behind them and pulls her to him, runs his hands from her shoulders down to her bottom, seeking the thrill he's been waiting for, but finding fear instead, coming off her body, or his, and a resistance from her bones that is out of proportion to her small skeleton. "What?" he says again. They sit on the edge of the bed. On the dresser, a half-empty pint of Old Grand-Dad. He picks it up. "What is this for?"

"My nerves," she says.

"You're nervous?" He puts the bottle back and pulls Lily closer. Now he can smell the bourbon. They haven't even kissed yet. "About me?"

"What am I doing here?" she asks. "What are we doing?"

"What are we doing? We're together. We're getting married."

She swipes at her eyes and wipes her hands on her dress. "It's all different."

"Thank God," he says. He'd like to take a swig from the bottle himself, but he's already light-headed from too many cigarettes and not enough food. And he's never known Lily to take a drink in her life. He lies back on the bed and pulls her on top of him. He kisses her, even though her mouth tastes sour. He tries to take her belt off, but gives up and takes his own belt off instead. Lily unbuttons one button of her dress and stops.

"Come on." He tries to sound lighthearted. "We got catching up to do."

She sighs and sits up and undresses matter-of-factly down to her cream-colored slip. Louis wonders if all the imaginary sex he had at McClellan was even with Lily, or if she was a stand-in for all girls, any girl. He takes off his tie and shirt. She touches his chest, his stomach, but without desire, fingers trembling. He puts her hand on his waistband and she dutifully opens his trousers and slips her hand inside. He is already hard. She pulls her hand away as if stung by a scorpion. He closes his eyes. He can't quite believe things are not unfolding as they did in his dreams these many months. He tries to put her hand back, but she sits up again and turns from him. One of her slip straps falls down.

"Okay, look." She tugs the strap back over her shoulder. "The truth is, I'm pregnant."

For a moment, Louis is confused. He wants to say, *No, it's Ruth who is pregnant.* Having known no pregnant women in his life, it's absurd that he should encounter two in one day. "You are?"

"I'm sorry. I never should have come here."

"Who got you pregnant?"

"Mama said I should come here and marry you and pretend it's yours."

"Whose is it?" he asks.

"And I thought I would, but now I can't."

"Are you sure?" He looks at her skinny frame and flat stomach. "Did a doctor say?"

"Yes. It's only eight weeks or something. It'll probably be so pale that not even you would believe it was yours."

"Why? Was it a white man? What do you mean 'not even me'?"

"I never should have come here and if you'll just give me the fare home I'll leave and we'll forget it."

"Why can't this white man pay your fare?" In his fury, he tries to picture Lily with some other man. The teller at the Iberville bank in his cheap brown suit. The fat Cajun who employs Lily's mother. The Greek iceman with the barrel chest. Lily's legs wrapped around each one in turn. Why had this never occurred to him? Yes, he visited a few prostitutes, but Lily was supposed to wait. "Why can't Mr. Big Shot pay your fare?"

She covers her face and starts crying again into her hands.

Louis zips his pants closed and takes the ninety-six dollars from his pocket. "This is all I have."

She lowers her hands and takes the whole wad. "Thank you," she sniffs.

Louis grabs it back. He peels off a twenty and puts it on the dresser. "This will get you back," he says, although he knows it is not enough. He stands up and puts on his shirt.

"I've got to eat, too," she says.

He finds a ten and adds it to the twenty. "So do I." He stuffs his tie and the remaining money in his pocket.

*   *   *

He finds a pay phone a few blocks over, flips through the book for cabs, calls and asks for a pickup at the Woolworth's. Big spokes of California sun poke through the leafy trees as he climbs the metal stairs and knocks on Ruth's door. The long, warm day will find Louis hitchhiking east out of the Sacramento Valley, over Echo Summit and down into the level blue light of the Lake Tahoe Basin and the raggedy edge of Carson City, Nevada. The casinos start as soon as you cross the state line. The stakes get higher. The poker players get wilier. But he will learn.

He tries the door, and it opens easily. Ruth is asleep on her back, looking as if she has not stirred since he left. Her big belly rises and falls under the blanket. When he clicks the door shut, her eyes open fast. "What's wrong?" she says.

"Nothing. It's Louis."

She pushes up on her elbows and looks at him.

"You were right," he says. "She's not coming."

"I'm sorry, Sergeant Paradiso." She closes her eyes and lies back.

"Call me Louis." He goes to the bed and picks her up, thin mattress and all. "I should have done this before," he says. "You are going to a hospital."

"No I'm not." It is not much of a protest. Her face is shiny and drained of color. She rests her head against his shoulder. He kisses the part in her hair.

"Don't get any ideas," she says.

He has lifted flour sacks and crates of potatoes that weighed as much as Ruth, but he has never carried them down a flight of stairs. He angles her out the door to the landing. Looks down. Takes the first step. Rebalances. A cab pulls up to the curb and the driver—a black man with iron-gray hair—gets out. At the bottom step, Louis nods to him. The driver eyes Ruth and says, "I don't drive no drunks."

"Open the back," Louis barks in his best sergeant's voice. He manages to get Ruth laid out, mattress and all, on the back seat.

By the time the two men settle into the front, the driver has figured out the pregnancy and softened up. "Your first kid?" His big-knuckled fingers have a light touch on the steering wheel.

"She's a friend. Where's the closest hospital?"

They come to a stop sign at the end of the block. "You don't want the closest." The driver's eyes, tired but kind, scan Louis's face for understanding.

Louis nods. "Well, take us where we need to go."

They cut across town to Sacramento County General, a mammoth stone building surrounded by old oaks, with the year 1880 carved over its front pillars. The driver is careful, quiet, a veteran of these situations. He pulls into a circular driveway. "Emergency room?" he asks.

Louis looks back at Ruth. "Don't forget, I can walk," she says. "I want to walk in the front door."

Inside, an older white lady sits at a desk in the cavernous lobby and smiles at them. She wears a smart gray suit and red lipstick. Louis hangs back and Ruth walks to the desk. For the first time, he notices that she is still wearing her white socks and no shoes. How could he have forgotten her shoes? The woman talks to Ruth and hands her papers and a pencil and points to a little room behind her. After Ruth goes in there, Louis approaches. "I want to pay her bill," he says.

"Sir, I don't know what the bill will be."

Louis takes all his cash, even the coins and the pelican, from his pockets and stacks it on the desk. "Would this be enough?"

"Sir, I don't know." She picks up the pelican, admires it, and puts it back.

"I just want to help. She's a friend."

"Well, you can go in there." The woman tilts her head toward the little room.

He scoops up the money. Ruth sits at a table, frowning down at the papers. "Should I put Hideo as the father?" she asks.

"Yes."

She hesitates. "I would be lying."

"Do it anyway."

Ruth writes the name and looks at it. "I'll put 'deceased.'" She adds the word.

"What was he like?" Louis asks.

Ruth raises her gaze to the milk-glass light globe hanging from the ceiling. "He was graceful," she says. "Walking, moving—he had, I don't know—" she looks at him "—no friction." Louis nods. "He could do big math problems in his head. He could make ya-kisoba. When he asked me to marry him, he cried." She frowns back down at the papers. "I never told that to anybody."

"What about his mom and pop?"

Ruth puts a hand on either side of the baby. "I'm too ashamed," she says.

"Can you find them?"

"I think so."

Louis places the money on the table.

"Oh no you don't," Ruth says.

"It might help."

She shakes her head. Closes her eyes as if to see more clearly into the future. Finally she says, "It must be a loan."

"Okay. A loan."

"How will I find you?" Ruth asks.

"I don't know," Louis says. "How will I find you?"

"I don't know."

"So it's a gift." Louis pushes the money a little closer.

The woman in the suit appears in the doorway. "All set?"

Ruth scrapes the chair back and pushes herself up.

"Good luck." Louis offers his hand.

She comes around the table and puts her arms around him, though she must turn sideways to do so. Standing on tiptoe, she kisses the corner of his mouth. "Take care of yourself, Sergeant."

"Call me Louis, would you?"

"Louis," she says.

Outside, the driver paces by the cab and looks up when Louis approaches. "Do we take the bed back?" he asks.

"Damn, I haven't paid you. I just gave her all my money."

The driver shrugs. "Don't matter."

Louis holds up the pelican. "I could pay you with my lucky charm."

"I can't take a guy's lucky charm." But he takes the pelican anyway and looks at it. "Nice." He returns it to Louis's palm. "There's no charge. I'll take you back."

"Could you maybe take me to the edge of town?"

"Which edge?"

"East."

"Sure."

As they pull away from the hospital, the driver asks Louis if he saw action in the Pacific.

"Nah," he says. "I was a cook. Stateside."

"Glad you made it through, anyhow." The driver lights a cigarette and offers the pack. Louis takes one and lights it.

The sun is well up now, streaming through the pitted windshield. Louis flips down the visor as they turn east toward the city limits.

8

The Empire Pool

When I was nineteen, my fiancé died. He died for England on May 10, 1943, in a mortar attack southwest of Tunis. For the next four years I stayed home in Cornwall, crying in the bath every morning and kissing Lawrence's photograph every evening. Then I decided to pull myself together and save the world.

I joined the army of English girls who converted their pre-war romantic desires into post-war committee work. By age twenty-four, I was an old hand. Public hygiene, solid fuel, labourers' safety. I had studied them all. I wanted to eradicate hunger, sterilize water, and modernize factories. I wanted every refugee in a safe home and every worker in a proper trade union. I volunteered for every committee, congress, and women's league that came my way, and there was no end to them. I suppose I still wanted to marry and start a family. But with all those thousands dead, it seemed another form of selfishness—like wanting sugar or petrol during rationing—to want a husband all to oneself.

On August 5, 1948, I traveled from Landsdowne, our family estate in Cornwall, to London for yet another conference: the Women's Congress on the Workplace. London was hosting the Olympic Games that summer. The city would be thick with celebrities, international dignitaries, foreign athletes, and exotic guests.

Before leaving home, I begged my older brother Rodney to come with me and do something useful. But he was too busy becoming a dipsomaniac and running with a crowd he called artists and our father called fruits. Rodney was our sole male heir—a male heir with no desire to carry on the family's mining interests in Cornwall. So, along with saving the world, it would fall to me to keep the winders and compressors and cassiterite separators of McAuley Tin Works roaring for another generation.

I stuffed a mottled brown cardboard binder in my bag—*Copper, Tin, Coal: A UK Survey*—and kissed my brother goodbye. Having seen too much American cinema, he saluted me with his morning gin and orange juice and said, "Go to it, Carrington. Knock 'em dead."

I had adored Rodney my whole life, and now he was simply breaking up. In the war he had done bomb disposal for the Royal Engineers, defusing unexploded mines and bombs from the airfields of England to the bridges along the Rhine. He lost most of his mates in the process. It had shattered his nerves and transformed him from the brilliant, happy lad I grew up with into a cynic intent upon pub-crawls and carousal.

My journey was dreadful. Crowded trains, late connections, unbearable heat. When I arrived at five o'clock that afternoon,

London sweltered under a blanket of copper-coloured air. I taxied to the Hotel Alexander, registered, and went looking for my fellow Congresswomen. I discovered two older ladies in a dim hallway, valiantly distributing pamphlets from a table draped with the faded banner of the Women's Congress on the Workplace. They greeted me with weary smiles, their face powder collecting into creases, their eyes sweetly sympathetic. After fussing through a box of loose papers, they found my committee assignment for the next day. Then they advised me to obtain a cup of tea.

The hotel tearoom was an overly warm octagonal solarium of faintly sooty glass. Red hibiscus and orange bird-of-paradise drooped amidst dense, green patterns of thick leaves. It all made me think of Lawrence. He had studied botany before he was called up. Even from the deserts of North Africa he wrote about plants. Once he sent tiny dried flowers sealed in cigarette-packet cellophane. At all events, I was relieved to sit under a Kaffir lime and order tea and sandwiches.

After a moment or two, I watched a man enter the tearoom. He was perhaps thirty years old, not tall, but conspicuous nonetheless. I imagined him a celebrity of some sort, a Spanish film star or Olympic gymnast from Brazil. I was certain he was not British. Not only because of his light brown skin—the shade and smoothness of which reminded me of the walnut-crème nougat candies I lusted after as a child—but because of his bearing. He was too confident and too filled out to be a Brit in 1948. Since the war, we all had a battered, twitchy, bloodless cast. This fellow was vital, his energy barely contained within his beautifully tailored suit. He appeared at home in the heat and humidity, standing there with the blackish-green fronds of a banana tree arcing over his head.

To my astonishment, his gaze rested on me. I became aware of my good silk blouse sticking to my back. And the train journey had played hell with my hair. The man strode directly to my table, inclined his head in a courteous little bow, and said, "Hi. Are you Miss Carrington McAuley?"

"Yes. Why?" I'm afraid I sounded abrupt. I resented his being good-looking, resented his American accent, resented that dreadful word *Hi*. Cufflinks of hammered silver peeped from his jacket cuffs.

"Okay if I join you?"

Whatever stunned smile I displayed he must have taken for consent. I was beset with contradictory feelings—wanting him to like me, wanting him to leave, wanting him to be Lawrence.

"Those gals by the banner told me a fellow worker was in here," he said. "We've been thrown together."

I had no idea what he meant. I was admiring the contrast between his starched white collar and his brown skin.

He pulled a paper from his jacket pocket and recited, "'Health and Safety Hazards in Rock, Sea, and Underground Mines.'"

"Oh, the committee," I said. "Yes. My family own the McAuley Tin Works in Cornwall. I'm to represent them."

"Lucky for McAuley Tin Works." This should have been the silliest sort of flattery, except he said it with utter solemnity. He introduced himself as Ramiro Delgado. Later I would learn the music of his full name: Jorge Salvador Ramiro Delgado y Cortés. Later I would learn he was thirty-two years old and traced his ancestry back to the Spanish conquistador, Hernán Cortés. At present, I learned he was from Texas. He was quick to add his parents were born in Mexico. He owned mines in Mexico, Bolivia, and Honduras. Mostly silver, he said, plus some nickel and "a few gems." He had come to London to see a diver named Joaquín Capilla Pérez, who was competing for Mexico in the Olympics.

I felt trapped beneath Mr. Delgado's unyielding gaze, like a butterfly in a killing bottle. I unfolded my serviette and couldn't resist dabbing at my forehead. "Isn't it like a jungle in here?" I said.

He smiled, showing strong American teeth. "I guess you've never been in a jungle."

The waiter arrived with my tea and sandwich tray. I offered Mr. Delgado a cucumber sandwich. He declined with a slight raise of his blunt fingers. I took one for myself—I was famished—and bit into it. He watched me as though my eating a cucumber sandwich were an amusement he had traveled miles to witness.

I examined the sandwich out of sheer nervousness. "Oh dear," I said, "they've used mayonnaise. I suppose butter is not available." I never should have said anything so ridiculous if his steady brown eyes hadn't made me uneasy. Before I could stop him, he held the tray aloft and motioned for the waiter.

"No. Please—" I said. But the waiter had scurried over.

"Miss McAuley wants butter on the sandwiches," he said.

"No, really, it's fine." The tray was already gone.

"Why shouldn't you have what you want?" he asked, leaning urgently across the table.

"We're accustomed to it," I said, rather defensively. "The war. Butter and things. We didn't have them."

"That's over now, isn't it?"

"Not entirely. And the sandwiches were fine."

"You should have what you want. That's important. I mean, for a young lady."

"No, it isn't." I did not like having a man who looked like a prince and probably owned half the metal ore in Central America telling me I should be selfish. "What is important is for people to work together, sacrifice together."

"Is that why you joined this club?"

"Mr. Delgado, please. It is not a club. It is a Women's Congress. We are joined together here, trying to repair the damages of war. Terrible damages to our country. Perhaps you don't understand."

"Oh, I understand, Miss McAuley. Trust me."

I had insulted him, which made me feel dreadful. After all, I had spent the war in relative safety in Cornwall, despite losing

Lawrence, despite the rationing and the constant reminders: the drone of Spitfires from the RAF base at Perranporth; the concrete anti-tank pimples dotting our lower meadows; the radar station bunker, a square grey castle sitting amidst barbed wire and anti-personnel mines on our bathing beach. What did I know of Mr. Delgado? My quick judgment of him brought back misgivings I often had about my committee work. Perhaps it was, as my brother Rodney sometimes implied, the indulgence of a well-heeled girl, a pointless salve to my conscience because half of Cornwall's miners were unemployed and McAuley Tin Works could not repair their lives and save them all.

"Forgive me, Mr. Delgado. It's just that I want to help rebuild England. There is much work to be done."

He not only paid for my tea, he invited me for supper. I could not bring myself to say yes. It felt disloyal. Disloyal to Lawrence, gone these five years, and disloyal to England as well. Must Americans forever rescue us? I knew we owed them a debt, but I detested their hubris. And I was still angry about the buttered sandwiches. Yes, they had magically appeared, and I had consumed them with a mixture of guilt and bliss. Because they seemed such an extravagance, I had convinced myself they would suffice as the evening meal. Lastly I thought with dismay of the mottled brown binder and its dreary survey of copper, tin, and coal, but I was determined to stay in my room that evening and read it.

Mr. Delgado did not insist. He could have persuaded me. Over the next 26 years I would rarely resist his powers of persuasion. He would persuade me to fall in love with him, persuade me to marry him, persuade me to move to Galveston, Texas, and persuade me to sell McAuley Tin Works—which had been in our family since 1604—for a vast amount of money. But that afternoon, after he escorted me back to reception and exited graciously, I was hoping I could avoid him at the next morning's meeting.

* * *

Held in the hotel's basement, in a room with grimy carpets and uncomfortable chairs and a persistent odour of stale, boiled tealeaves, the next morning's meeting was destined for a bad start. Like so many "women's conferences" I attended, the drudgery of organizing had been carried out by women and the capricious content of the meetings threatened to be dominated by men. In fact, of the thirty or so people on this committee, I was one of only three women. Mr. Delgado arrived at the last moment, and, in what I considered yet another instance of American audacity, he asked the man sitting next to me in the front row to move so he could join me. The poor blighter nodded and scurried to the back.

One of the older ladies from the day before welcomed us with fluttering heartfelt thanks—she even singled out Mr. Delgado as one of our esteemed American guests—but she had neither the authority nor the gumption to prevent a pushy Australian man from rising and launching a monologue on acid heap leaching of chalcopyrites. Exactly the type of special interest that threatened to take over so many meetings in which the most fundamental objectives had yet to be decided.

Despite the Australian's pomposity, he had lovely light brown hair, the same colour and cow-licked unruliness as Lawrence's. I remembered the first time I touched Lawrence's hair. A springtime day at Landsdowne, hillsides pink with heather, fresh wind off the sea. We were playing croquet on the back lawn when he suddenly dropped his mallet and pulled me into an embrace. He smelled of Pears soap and cigarettes. I was eighteen and so mad for him that when he kissed me, my thought was, "At last I am whole." A schoolgirl notion, but even now, as the Australian droned on about zinc and manganese, tears stung my eyes.

I pushed aside memories of Lawrence and tried to jot notes for my own monologue on the need for an agenda of broader topics—proper workers' insurance and workers' compensation, for example. Before I could speak, another man took the floor and began rambling in an unintelligible Welsh accent about something—bauxite, perhaps.

Completely frustrated, I stood and blurted, "Forgive me, but we are wasting valuable time." The Welshman stopped. The bright red spot on each of his cheeks grew brighter and his florid nostrils flared. "We haven't yet set an agenda," I persisted. People behind me cleared throats and rustled papers. "What about overarching issues like compensation for accidents? Insurance for miners' families?"

The Welshman was too flustered to speak, but the Australian stood up and took his part. "Madam, this gentleman had the floor."

"No one has the floor," I protested. "We've not even elected a chairman."

"Are you saying you want the job?" he asked.

"Yes," I said. "I have experience leading discussions of this type."

He looked out over the audience. "Oh, this girl has *experience*," he called out. "Is she the chairman? All in favor?"

No one spoke. I stared at a huge, horrid painting behind the Australian—a sea battle, perhaps Queen Elizabeth's ships going against the Spanish Armada—wondering if England would ever return to her former glory.

Before the Australian could finish his mock vote, Mr. Delgado stood up. "Wait a minute," he said. "She has a point."

"Are you her husband?"

"Of course not. Her family owns mines and so does my family, and we are business associates."

I admired this answer, even if it weren't quite true.

"So what are you proposing?" The Australian folded his thick arms.

"The same thing Miss McAuley is proposing. An agenda of topics for all miners, not just certain interests."

"Make *him* chairman," someone called out.

"You don't need me as chairman," Mr. Delgado said amiably. "I know for a fact Miss McAuley is perfectly capable."

Did all Americans lie this smoothly? Was it yet another thing they were better at than Brits?

"Well then, co-chairmen," the same voice suggested.

And so for the remaining two hours of the meeting, Mr. Delgado and I sat in the front and directed the discussion. Or rather he directed it and I pretended I had an equal voice. A pattern quickly emerged in which my words would be greeted by silence and chilly looks; then Mr. Delgado would rephrase what I had said, as if interpreting from female to male language, with the added weight of an American accent. All the while, wan daylight filtered through the smudged windows at ceiling level, making me somehow angry and sleepy at the same time. When we adjourned at one o'clock, we had managed to draw up a list of urgent topics and a few resolutions. It felt like progress, despite the fact that actual subject matter had yet to be broached. That would take place at our second meeting, the next morning at ten.

After we adjourned, the Australian buttonholed Mr. Delgado and I fled upstairs to the hotel lobby. Whom should I see at the front desk but my brother Rodney. He was leaning over a slate countertop immersed in conversation with the concierge.

When he saw me he cried out, "Carrington! There you are. Excellent!"

"Rodney?"

"I've taken your advice." He gripped my shoulders. "I've come to make myself useful. You may tell your little conference that Rodney McAuley is here to set the world right."

He looked well. Sober, pressed, and combed. His blue eyes were bright and his always-pale skin had some healthy colour to it.

"When did you arrive?" I asked. "How did you travel?"

"My dear, I have connections, as you know. I caught a ride in a wonderful motorcar. Quite extravagant."

"Whose motorcar?"

"Where shall we lunch?" he asked. "They've no more rooms here," he went on. "God knows where I'll find—" He broke off and looked over my shoulder, then back at me. "A lovely man is staring at us," he whispered.

When I turned, Mr. Delgado strode toward us. I introduced my brother. Rodney gave me a quick, questioning, what-have-we-been-up-to glance and shook Mr. Delgado's hand. "Won't you lunch with us?" Rodney asked.

"Yes," Mr. Delgado said, "but you must be my guests."

"Even better," Rodney said.

I did not object. There seemed no end to Mr. Delgado's largesse. We walked to a restaurant in Kensington High Street and he promptly ordered champagne.

"Excellent!" cried Rodney. "What are we celebrating?"

Mr. Delgado filled my glass. "Your sister's valiant efforts at our committee meeting."

Rodney groaned. "Oh, that's far too boring."

"Shall we toast your diver?" I suggested.

"You have a diver?" Rodney was intrigued.

"He is Mexico's diver," Mr. Delgado explained. "In the Olympic Games. Joaquín Capilla Pérez. My family knows his family."

"Mr. Delgado came all this way expressly to see him."

"Please," Mr. Delgado said. "You have to call me Ramiro."

"What charming names you Americans have," Rodney said. We all reestablished ourselves on first-name footing.

"To Joaquín Capilla Pérez." I raised my glass.

"Long may he dive." Rodney raised his.

If the butter had induced guilt, the champagne would surely send me straight to hell. As would the expensive lunch we all ordered. Rodney asked for oysters, and even I could not resist the beefsteak, which Ramiro approved of with an enthusiastic nod, ordering the same for himself.

"When does the diving take place?" Rodney asked.

"The first event is tomorrow morning, I'm afraid. Ten o'clock." Ramiro looked at me.

It took a moment for this information to sink in. "But what about our meeting?" I asked. "Our meeting is at ten o'clock." I realized this meant I'd be facing the committee alone.

"Your meeting?" Rodney was horrified. "Why would he listen to ladies'-congress puffery when he can watch this Capilla chap?"

"Joaquín Capilla Pérez," Ramiro said.

"Yes. Joaquín Capilla Pérez," Rodney repeated, as if he knew the man. "His name alone makes it worth missing a meeting. By the way, can you get us in? To the diving?"

"Rodney, please. He has been far too generous already."

"Of course I can," Ramiro said. "Will you come? Both of you?"

"Count me in." Rodney poured himself more champagne.

Our food arrived. All at once, my slab of beef looked wasteful and detestable. My appetite evaporated. I dreaded facing the committee without Mr. Delgado. But I was determined to try. "Forgive me, but I must rejoin the committee tomorrow. You saw how it was."

"Carrington," Ramiro said, "if you don't mind my saying, I don't hold out much hope for that group, in terms of it accomplishing anything."

"But we have to try. We have to begin somewhere."

"Carrie, start with your own life." Rodney downed an oyster and filled his glass yet again. "Have some fun."

"Rodney, there is work to do." Suddenly I detested him as well. "We can't all be playboys."

"We can't mourn dead fiancés forever, either," he shot back.

We never sniped at each other like this before the war. We had always been such good chums. I clenched my knife and fork. "You are drinking too much, Rodney. As usual."

"And you are becoming a stuffy old spinster at twenty-four. Do you think Lawrence wanted you to live like a nun?"

"Do not use his name to insult me."

"He's not Jesus Christ."

"He's closer than you."

A humiliating silence descended. Rodney continued with his oysters as if nothing had happened. I turned to Ramiro. "Forgive us," I said. "We're behaving abominably."

"Don't worry. You should've heard me and my brother go at it. I mean, when he was alive. He died in France."

"I'm so dreadfully sorry," I said.

"Very sorry," Rodney mumbled.

"As for me," Ramiro added, "the army didn't want me. Scarlet fever. Apparently it leaves its mark on your heart."

"My fiancé died in Tunisia," I said. "I miss him terribly."

"It was five years ago, Carrie."

"Rodney, you've been cruel enough."

"Yes," he admitted. "I am sorry." To show he meant it, he refused the glass of cognac that Ramiro offered after the meal. Ramiro paid what must have been an enormous bill. We left the restaurant and returned to the Hotel Alexander in silence.

* * *

I assumed I would never see Ramiro Delgado again. The committee meetings would extend over the next three days, but I imagined he would not return to any of them. Another American trait—follow your own programme, regardless of commitments or inconvenience to others. Rodney asked me for supper that night. I was still angry with him and I refused. I knew then his claim of doing something useful was false. He would gad about London until it bored him. Then he would seek fresh entertainment elsewhere. I returned to my room, resigned to another evening of study before facing the committee on my own.

Much later that night I awoke to the sound of thumping on my door. I had fallen asleep, still dressed and with the lamp on. The brown binder—*Copper, Tin, Coal*—lay open on my chest.

The room was hot. I was disoriented. I called out to ask who was there.

"It's your darling brother," Rodney sang out, in his loudest, most drunken voice.

I opened the door. He looked like a gangster from an American film, with his suit jacket hooked on his thumb and a bottle of gin dangling from the other hand.

"Oh, Rodney."

"I must talk to you." He tried to articulate each solemn word, but he couldn't stop grinning his old boyhood grin. And there was someone behind him in the shadows of the hallway. He was a very fair, very young man, young enough to have two or three spots on his face, but he was wearing an immaculate dinner jacket. He eyed me quickly, then looked away and stepped farther into the gloom.

"Who is that?"

"That's a friend. That's Nicky. He's a friend."

"The motorcar?" I guessed.

"Nicky indeed possesses a fine motorcar. Don't you, Nick?"

No response.

Rodney turned and handed Nicky the bottle. "I'll be back straightaway," he told him.

He came into my room and closed the door. I still had the brown binder in my hand. Rodney took it from me, riffled the pages, and read aloud: "'Commercial possibilities vary with the initial cost outlay of sinking deep pits, depending on the expenses accrued. . . .'" He slapped the book shut.

"Really, Carrington, you've got to pack this in."

"Pack what in?"

"This mission you're on."

"And do what? Drink and pick up boys?"

"Now that hurt." He sat on the bed and let himself topple over, pressing the binder to his heart. "I'm deeply wounded." He was still grinning.

"You should not have come here, Rodney."

"That Ramiro chap likes you," he said to the ceiling. "He's quite lovely as well."

"He does not like me. All Yanks act like that."

"You don't even know any Yanks."

"Well, they shouldn't traipse in here with their dollars and their silver mines and pretend everything's wonderful."

"Why not?" Rodney flung his arms across the bed. "Let's pretend! Maybe wonderful will happen."

"And maybe it won't." But already my heart told me otherwise. Ramiro Delgado was, after all, everything I had dreamed of back in those pre-war days, when we all felt free to dream. Charming, mysterious. Apparently wealthy. Even sexually attractive, although I hardly dared think the words. I had never had sexual relations with a man. The closest I had come was sitting on a bed like this with Lawrence in a hotel room in Bristol, just before he left for military training. That was the pinnacle of our intimacy—sitting on a bed. Kissing. We didn't make love, though we came that close. I made him wait.

Rodney startled me from my daydream by sitting up and slowly ripping a page from my binder. "Quit trying to do the proper thing for England." He tore the page in half and then into quarters, then eighths. "Lawrence is dead. Do something for yourself." He let the pieces flutter down. It was a graph of a century's worth of coal exports.

Much to my consternation, I began weeping. Rodney folded me in his arms and kissed my hair. "Now look, Carrington. Take Nicky-boy out there," he said.

"You take him," I sniffed.

"Oh, I will. But he's patriotic, just like you. Rule Britannia, that's Nick. And you know how he serves his country? He serves his country by saying, 'Nicky-boy is no good for England or anything else if he's unhappy.'"

"Rodney, you've found a very convenient philosophy."

"It's what I learned in the war, Carrie."

"Philosophy?"

"Well, no." He fumbled behind him on the bed for his jacket. "Perhaps I learned the opposite of philosophy."

"Rodney, whatever is the opposite of philosophy?"

"My dear, the opposite of philosophy is terror."

"Terror? You mean fear of death?" I asked.

"I don't think so. Not those brave, I'm-your-man Royal Engineers. We all stopped fearing death early on."

"Fear of what, then?"

"Of never having lived."

* * *

The vaulted ceiling of Wembley Stadium was almost lost in the bright silver light that streamed through banks of windows high above tiered galleries. Row upon row of spectators fanned themselves with programmes that flashed blue white blue white. In the centre of it all, the Empire Pool was a flat turquoise rectangle. At one end, a tower of iron scaffolding supported the diving boards and platforms.

As we entered, Ramiro took my hand—a simple gesture that evoked sensations for me as vast as the stadium itself, as if I *had* saved the world and now it was laid at my feet for me to enjoy. Oh, there was guilt too. Another part of me felt like a little girl playing hooky. But how quickly I allowed Ramiro—his tailored suit, his warm hand—to bestow upon me his unfamiliar brand of confidence. Maybe this was how all Americans felt as they went about ordering butter and consuming beefsteak and rescuing nations.

Rodney, who had brought the silent Nicky along, kept sneaking me knowing grins and quick V-for-Victory signs. He was taking all the credit for prying me away from my meeting and pushing me into Ramiro's magic sphere. And it was magic, the way Ramiro produced passes from his slim leather wallet so that the four of us—Ramiro, Rodney, Nicky, and I—sat like the royal family in a row of seats behind the judges for the diving competition.

Joaquín Capilla Pérez, who that day would win a bronze medal for Mexico in the ten-meter platform dive, paced alongside the pool. He noticed Ramiro on one of his nervous crossings and smiled at him. Capilla Pérez was twenty-five years old, but looked like a teenager. His pointy shoulders angled out above his slender waist and red swim trunks. His taut brown back was a triangle of confined energy. Before his event, he joined the other divers in the pool for their two minutes of acclimation, treading water or swimming a few strokes.

Ramiro put his arm round my shoulders and spoke directly into my ear. "Joaquín noticed you," he said. "He's wondering why I am here with such a stunning Englishwoman."

I shook my head and tried not to smile. As far as I could tell, Mr. Capilla Pérez had not looked at me at all.

"I'll talk to him later," Ramiro added. "I'll tell him we're falling in love."

I wanted both to believe and to protest this terrifying statement, but at that moment Joaquín Capilla Pérez's name and dive were announced, in English, then French. He climbed to the top of the platform and stood poised, shimmying his shoulders and dripping water from his fingertips. He stepped to the edge and pushed off. Somehow he suspended himself high above the water for the length of time needed to press his forehead to his knees and carve three and a half languid circles in the silvery air. Each somersault whipped out a perfect arc of shiny drops from his thick black hair. Then, as if it were his decision and not gravity's, he opened the blade of his body toward the water and pierced its placid blue surface.

Applause. Echoed shouts from every corner of the galleries. Next to me, Ramiro leapt to his feet, cheering, fists raised over his head. On my other side, Rodney, shouting *Bravo*, hugged me. I looked over his shoulder at Nicky, who smiled at me with his mild eyes. When Rodney let me go, Ramiro took me in his arms. He was laughing. Then he kissed me. It was a hungrier kiss than poor Lawrence had ever mustered, and, even in the midst of it, I had the terrible, brief vision of his falling in the desert. Perhaps the war ended for me when I gripped the fine wool of Ramiro's suit and kissed him back. I didn't care who saw us. I wanted to celebrate.

9

Castle Bravo

Carrington raised the silver coffeepot and forced herself to smile. She poured coffee violently enough to splash a few drops onto Alicia Parker's pink dress. She didn't like Alicia—or her boring husband John—but she was determined to play the darling hostess. Behind her fake smile, she was worried about her daughter Iris and lusting after several things at once: cigarettes, sex, sleep.

Her husband Ramiro had invited these people. John Parker would probably win a Texas state senate seat next month in the 1960 elections. He'd be able to help Ramiro's family firm, Delgado Mines. So if that meant two hours of small talk on the terrace, watching the Parkers work their way through steaks and salads, then Carrington would do it. But now, over coconut crème pie and coffee, she regretted the waste of a beautiful Galveston evening, a soft coral sunset, the shining blue Gulf in the distance.

"Did you make the pie yourself?" Alicia Parker asked.

"No, Pilar made the pie," Carrington said wearily.

"Oh, that's right," Alicia said. "Your Mexican."

* * *

From her bedroom window on the second floor, Iris Delgado—ten years old, with dried-salt tear tracks on her cheeks—glared down on her parents' dinner party. She heard the fat lady in pink call their cook Pilar a *Mexican*. She wanted to yell *Nicaraguan!* but then they'd know she was watching. For the hundredth time that day she took up the round mirror with the blue plastic handle and looked at her hair. Fresh tears filled her eyes. Her hair poked this way and that in ragged brown patches all over her head.

* * *

On the terrace, Ramiro watched his wife pour the coffee, admiring her trim figure in the ivory linen sheath, her tan arms bare to the shoulder, her naturally curly, naturally yellow short hair. He loved Carrington, no matter her mood, and the anger he detected behind the coffee-splashing excited him. When she got mad and bored like this she liked to burn it off with sex. He imagined her telling the Parkers—in her charming British accent—to *bugger off*. Then the two of them would obliterate the day's crises with backed-up lust. They would forget that their daughter Iris had gone a little crazy that morning. They would forget that their hired man, Louis Paradiso, had come in after lunch saying he felt sick. Not exactly a crisis, but Ramiro wondered if the man could be drinking again. He was a good caretaker, and Ramiro counted on him to run their vast corner of Galveston, a spread of land dotted with pecan orchards, lemon groves, hay fields, and swampland.

"Now, how is that daughter of yours?" Alicia Parker asked.

Ramiro answered quickly, before Carrington could say anything. "We have two daughters, actually. Hannah is eight, and Iris is ten."

"Which one is a little bit odd?" Alicia's rosebud lips protruded lewdly to vacuum pie off her fork.

"Alicia, what kind of thing is that to say?" John Parker's voice, Ramiro realized, was as bland as his brown tie and brown crew cut and brown horn-rim spectacles.

Ramiro smiled. "Our daughters are just run-of-the-mill little girls," he said, wondering how to change the subject to government contracts and Delgado Mines. "Crying one minute, then dancing in front of *American Bandstand* the next."

Alicia scraped invisible remnants of pie crust from her plate. "But isn't one girl a special genius or something?"

Unlike you, Carrington wanted to say. But she let Ramiro handle it.

"Iris has skipped a couple of grades," he said.

* * *

Iris heard her name spoken down on the terrace and leaned toward the window again. More than anything she feared being called upon to come down and *shake hands.* She hated *shaking hands.* Or being touched by anyone except possibly her father. Well, Louis Paradiso, of course. She adored him. And her mother was okay, but way too fussy and now there was the hair disaster. Below, the pink lady was asking the usual questions about Iris being a genius.

* * *

In fact, at age ten, Iris could easily have been a high school senior, but the schools had balked at moving her beyond eighth grade. "Her sister Hannah, on the other hand," Ramiro was saying, "Hannah is your average third-grader."

"Where are they?" Alicia looked over her shoulder, as if Hannah or Iris might pop out from behind the potted palms.

"Hannah's at a slumber party," Carrington said. Hannah had flounced out of their Oldsmobile 88 and up the steps of her friend's house earlier that afternoon, carrying a box of Frankie Avalon and Bobby Darin 45's and grumbling that her sister Iris was *nuts*.

"And Iris is in her room," Carrington went on. "She's not feeling well."

"Oh, the poor little thing," Alicia said. "Does she have a summer cold?"

"Yes," Carrington lied. That was easier than the truth: that Iris had sequestered herself in her room after chopping off most of her hair that afternoon with paper doll scissors during a test of Galveston's air-raid sirens.

Iris's IQ did place her within the strange nation of genius, and neither Ramiro nor Carrington was sure how to cope with it. At two years old, Iris could read road signs, and by three she could memorize a third grade schoolbook in one sitting. She moved on to everything from Carrington's copies of *Vogue* to encyclopedias, dictionaries, novels, and the government mining reports she found in her father's office. It wasn't enough to skip grades or buy more advanced books or get a special pass at the Rice University libraries to keep her from getting bored. Iris was fragile, as if all her cerebral gifts had been gained at the price of resilience. Much of her knowledge terrified her, but she could not resist pursuing it: polio, iron lungs, killer bees, DDT, small pox, scorpions, earth-impact asteroids, airplane crashes, Gulf storm surges, and Texas tornadoes. She read up on all of it. But nothing terrified or obsessed her more than the bomb. She could quote the Hiroshima yield (20 kilotons TNT), the Nagasaki yield (21 kilotons), the atmospheric height of the Trinity mushroom cloud (8 miles), code names of US and Russian tests (Ivy Mike, Castle Romeo, Castle Bravo, Joe-1, Joe-4), crater sizes, generated wind speeds, death tolls. She knew the difference between fusion and fission, hydrogen bombs and atom bombs, and she had saved plans from *Life* magazine for a fallout shelter.

Carrington stacked their dessert plates onto a tray. Maybe if she cleared dishes, the Parkers would take the hint. As she stood with the tray she saw Louis Paradiso walking up from the gardens toward the terrace. He had on a blue suit with an open-necked white shirt. That was his uniform, Carrington knew, when he played blues guitar at a tavern in town.

Louis was forty-two years old, but he didn't look it. His eyes showed some age—wise and tired—but that was offset by his muscled shoulders and the smooth copper skin from his Chickasaw heritage. He didn't make much money with his music—only tips—but he loved playing.

"What's up?" Ramiro asked.

"I'll be taking the truck." Louis looked only to Carrington. "Okay?"

Carrington said, "Of course" in the same instant that Ramiro said, "I thought you were sick."

Louis buttoned the front of his suit jacket, then unbuttoned it. "It's just, I said I'd play up to Tino's," he said. "People expecting me."

"Women especially, I imagine," Carrington suggested, smiling at him, trying to draw him out. He gazed at her, giving away nothing. But Carrington knew he had girlfriends. He lived over the garage, and more than once she had heard him taking someone home in the truck as the sun came up. Otherwise, he took care of their land and kept to himself, except to spend time with Hannah and Iris. He loved showing them how to pick pecans or find pelican nests or trim oleanders.

"I won't stand for getting drunk," Ramiro put in.

"Ramiro, really." Carrington didn't want the Parkers to glimpse any rift in their domestic perfection. And Louis had given up drinking years ago when he came to work for them. He had never relapsed, as far as she knew.

"All right." Ramiro raised a hand, dismissing Louis.

Carrington called out, "Have yourself a good evening, Louis." But he was already back on the path toward the gardens.

"Is he a Nigra or a Mexican?" Alicia asked.

* * *

Chickasaw! Iris wanted to scream from her window. But she kept silent. The alibi of the summer cold was good. No shaking hands. But how long until the weirdoes finally left and until her mother finally took the bath she always took after guests, smoking a bunch of cigarettes in the tub, and how long before she—Iris—would have her father to herself and he would forgive her for cutting her hair?

"I just love your funny little accent," Alicia was saying to Carrington. "Now where all is it you're from?"

Great Britain! At her window, Iris crossed her arms and peered down in disgust. *England! Cornwall!*

* * *

That afternoon, the sirens hadn't so much registered on Iris's ears as entered her everywhere: through her eyes, mouth, ribcage and fingernails. She knew it was *only a test,* but her whole body trembled like a tuning fork until she couldn't tell if she was absorbing the sound or emitting it herself from sheer terror. Her sister Hannah, who sat on the floor cutting out paper doll clothes, had looked up when the sirens started, then went back to trimming the tabs on a wedding dress. Happy Hannah.

The sirens—those shrieks heralding the end of the world—were thirty seconds into their three-minute test when Iris grabbed the scissors and chopped a clump of her own shoulder-length brown hair off and let it fall to the floor.

What My Last Man Did

Hannah stared up at her. "I'm telling."

Iris reached around the back of her head for another clump and sawed that off too. Hannah ran down the hall, yelling for their mother.

While the sirens pealed the apocalypse, the handfuls of hair falling to the rug provided a strange safety. Something she could engineer herself, since nobody else seemed to care. Certainly not her school, with its duck-and-cover drills. Didn't they know anything? Didn't they know about Castle Bravo, an H-bomb test with a fireball four and a half miles wide? When you're about to be vaporized you don't hide under a Tinkertoy desk.

By the time Hannah dragged their mother in, most of Iris's hair was on the rug in a ragged circle around her chair. The sirens had ceased their keening and the air stood scrubbed and still in the aftermath. "Oh, Iris." Carrington gathered up handfuls of hair and dropped them into the wastebasket, fighting down guilt and anger. Guilt at her inability to understand this stranger who was her firstborn. Guilt that sometimes she liked Hannah better. Anger at Iris's impulsiveness, turning herself into a freak, and with the Parkers due in a couple of hours.

While her mother stood wringing her hands and staring into the wastebasket, Iris had wandered outside. It was midday and muggy, a Saturday in early October. In the heavy air, the low-tide smell from the south collided with the bougainvillea scent along the garden walls. Iris couldn't find her father—the person she counted on to absolve all sins—but she found Louis Paradiso in one of the sheds. He sat on an old footlocker, his Fender guitar on his lap, a small bottle of rye whiskey by his right foot. The guitar wasn't plugged in, but he practiced some tinny-sounding chords. He looked at her hair and said, "New style?"

Iris shrugged. "I didn't like the sirens."

"Me either," he said.

She pointed at the bottle. "Is that why you have *that*?"

"Nah," he said. He moved it behind the footlocker, embarrassed she had seen it and hoping she wouldn't tell her father. "Just feeling lonely."

"You're lonely?" Iris had thought loneliness was her sole dominion. "You have me." She sat next to him. "Even if I look like Frankenstein." She wanted to climb into his lap like she used to, but she knew she was too old for that. And the whiskey smell was foreign and somehow ominous. She cut him a sideways look.

"Okay," he said. "I had a drink."

Iris reached back for the bottle and held it to the light.

"A few drinks," he added. "So what?"

On top of the sirens, this was too much. *So what?* Louis didn't talk like that. And he wasn't supposed to drink. She wanted to say *I'm telling* in the whiny voice of her sister. She wanted her old hair back, right now, and she wanted the real Louis back. She wanted all sirens everywhere to be silent and all atomic explosions, past and future, to rewind into never-igniting chunks of uranium or plutonium and stay there. But for the moment, she took hold of the guitar's neck and tried to right the world with something familiar. She arranged her fingers into an A minor seventh. Louis had shown it to her the day before.

Louis strummed through the chord for her. He loved Iris but didn't feel like giving a guitar lesson. He patted her shoulder blades where they stuck out like chicken wings, hoping she would give up and leave. She was a skinny, gawky kid, burdened with brilliance. She bore some resemblance to her beautiful mother. The same wide-set eyes and fair English skin. He imagined Iris and her sister would both be stunners.

"Show me another chord," Iris said.

"Do you want me to trim this?" Louis touched a ragged patch over her left ear. "I can cut hair, you know." He didn't like her holding the bottle. He took it from her and tilted it to his lips, as if to prove he could do whatever he wanted. The Delgados didn't own him.

Iris smelled the whiskey again. "Leave me alone." She pushed his hand away from her hair and stood up. "You know what my mother would say?" She looked him up and down. "She'd say you're *pissed*."

"Look, Iris, don't tell, okay?" But Iris was already stomping out of the shed.

* * *

With the coconut crème pie finished, Ramiro steered John Parker into a conversation about Delgado Mines. He unfolded a map he had half hidden under his napkin. "This is where we're excavating some new veins in Bolivia. A lot of silver." He ran his finger along a mountain range and John Parker leaned forward politely.

"Could you show me the powder room?" Alicia asked.

Carrington led her inside from the terrace and pointed to the first-floor bathroom. Then she fled upstairs, lit a Newport from the cigarette-and-lighter stash she kept behind a philodendron on the landing, and went to Iris's room. "Honey?"

Iris looked up from her desk. "When are they leaving?" She had rubbed away the tear tracks and her cheeks were pink.

"Soon. How are you feeling?" Carrington dragged on her cigarette.

"Mom, it's a haircut. It doesn't *hurt*." She touched her temple where her scalp shone through, marble-white and vulnerable.

"I know." Carrington sighed. The cropped tufts made her daughter look like a cartoon cat stuck in a light socket. "But you were pretty upset."

"I'm fine now. I'm reading." Iris held up her innocent copy of *And Now Miguel*. It was a decoy. She had stashed the real book she was reading, the one that described nuclear bomb tests, in a drawer.

"Did you eat?" Carrington set her lighter on Iris's desk and tipped cigarette ash into her palm.

"Yes."

"Did you really?"

"Ask Pilar. I ate. I stuffed myself. Macaroni and cheese and a glass of milk and coconut crème pie. We might have a dairy product explosion."

Carrington smiled. She turned to leave, but heard someone on the stairs. She leaned over the bannister and saw the billowing pink skirt. "Yoo hoo!" Alicia called. "Are you girls up here?"

Carrington tried to find somewhere to stub out her cigarette and dump the ashes and close Iris's door and pretend nothing was happening all at the same time.

"I just have to meet this smart little girl." Alicia pushed past Carrington and into Iris's room. There was nothing to do with the cigarette but hold onto it. Carrington wanted to put it out in the metal wastebasket, but it was still half-full of hair.

"Iris, this is Mrs. Parker."

Iris stood and looked at the carpet. "Hi."

"Can you speak up?" Carrington said.

"Hi," Iris repeated.

"Why, whatever in the world happened to your hair?" Alicia blurted. She touched her own bubble-styled head, as if Iris's hair might threaten her own.

"We had a little accident," Carrington said.

"Or a little train wreck," Alicia said.

Iris raised her gaze to burn it into Alicia.

"Sweetie-pie, I could help you fix that." As Alicia reached out her stubby fingers, Carrington glimpsed, for a moment, what was about to happen. How Alicia would touch Iris. How Iris would lash out. How Alicia would be hurt. How soon-to-be State Senator

John Parker and his chubby, pink wife would leave in a huff. But at least they'd leave. Soon Carrington would have Ramiro to herself. She'd have his wonderful-smelling chest on top of her the moment these people cleared the driveway in their ugly orange Chrysler Imperial. She'd have the bedroom door locked and the sheets kicked on the floor and a long night of lovemaking and sleeping and waking up to more lovemaking.

With an animal yelp of fear, Iris slapped Alicia's hand away. And she kept on slapping, hands paddling the air like a furious two-year-old. She connected with a few slaps and scratches to Alicia's forearm, and one significant slap to her face, before the stunned Alicia could turn away.

"Why you little brat." Alicia pressed her hand to her cheek. "You vicious little—"

Carrington wedged herself between her daughter and Alicia. "Iris, sit down. Now."

Iris sat and swiveled back to her desk.

Carrington put her arm around Alicia's shoulders and led her back to the terrace, apologizing as they went, turning her head to take desperate drags from the still-burning cigarette.

* * *

They stood on the porch as the Parkers drove off. "I know," Ramiro said. "They're idiots. But we need him."

"I'm sorry," Carrington said. "I'll call Alicia tomorrow. Try to explain."

They stepped into the foyer, but the evening air felt so soothing that Ramiro left the door open and put his arms around his wife. Hours earlier, he had zipped the back of Carrington's linen sheath for her and kissed the nape of her neck. All evening he had wanted to pull the zipper back down and now he had his chance. He ran his hand inside the dress, over the soft skin of her back and under the edges of her bra.

"Daddy?" Iris stood on the stairs above them, watching. Ramiro dropped his hands. Carrington tugged the dress back over her shoulder.

Ramiro took in the haircut for the first time. He kept his voice neutral. "Iris, isn't it your bedtime?"

"I want to show you something." Iris held a piece of paper.

"Mrs. Parker was very upset, Iris." Ramiro secretly slipped his hand back inside Carrington's dress.

"Mrs. Parker is stupid." Iris started down the stairs, clomping hard on each step. "Look at this."

"Go—to—bed, Iris," Carrington said.

"No." Iris came closer. "This is Castle Bravo." She showed them a black and white aerial photograph of a mushroom cloud. "They messed it up," she said. "They didn't calculate for lithium-7."

"Iris, not now!" Carrington pulled away from Ramiro and twisted her arms behind her, trying to find the bottom of the zipper.

"The yield was fifteen megatons, the biggest ever." Iris held the paper up to her father's face. "It poisoned everybody, all the island people."

"Where did you get this?" Ramiro took it and read the caption: *Castle Bravo, Bikini Atoll, 1 March 1954.*

"I cut it out of a book," Iris said.

He stared at the glowing jellyfish cap of the hydrogen explosion, swelling above a layer of cloud cover. An elliptical saucer of brilliant light hovered like a fifty-mile-wide lampshade over the mushroom top.

"That's why I cut my hair." Iris pointed from the picture to her head.

Carrington gave up on the zipper. "And turned yourself into more of a freak than you already were," she snapped.

"What?" Ramiro looked at her.

"Well, she is." Carrington's mouth was taut and white. "Isn't she?"

Iris stood there fingering a tuft of hair. "I'm not a freak." The hurt in her eyes slowly condensed into fury. She raised her small fist and landed a weak blow on Carrington's shoulder. Then she stepped closer, grabbed the top of her mother's dress and dragged it down, digging in a fingernail hard enough to scratch a line from Carrington's collarbone to the swell of her breast above the bra. "There," she said, satisfied, still gripping the fabric, watching the scratch redden.

Carrington's jaw hardened and she hissed in a deep breath. Ramiro hugged Iris from behind, pried her fingers off the dress, and pinned her arms. "Iris, Iris, Iris," he whispered into her impossible hair.

In the small silence that followed they heard quick steps on the porch. Louis reached the doorway, smiling. "I saw the door open, and—" He stopped as he took in Carrington, grappling again with her dress; Ramiro, holding Iris with one hand and reaching to help his wife with the other; Iris, wriggling out of her father's grasp, saying, "I hate everybody," as she stooped to pick up a photograph from the floor. Louis tried to put the scene together. "Everything okay?" He knew it was not, but he needed to hide his anguish at seeing Carrington's bare shoulder, pale chest, the white straps. Now he heard her breath—loud, hard, almost sexual.

Iris studied the photograph. "They really messed up," she muttered to herself.

Louis held out his hand. "Let me take you up, sweetheart." Iris shook her head.

Ramiro shot Louis a pleading look. Louis got his arm around Iris and steered her toward the stairs. "Come on," he said. She trailed along with him, dragging her feet.

Ramiro called after them. "I'll take you to a beauty parlor on Monday, Iris."

"I hate beauty parlors," Iris yelled back.

Behind them, Louis heard Ramiro say, "Darling, calm down." They must have turned toward the kitchen, but Carrington said loudly, "I don't want to calm down."

In Iris's room, Louis closed the door.

"Are you drunk?" Iris asked.

"Maybe a little," he confessed.

"I'm telling."

Her mother's Ronson lighter was still on the desk, next to a fat, cloth-bound library book. Iris took up the lighter and snapped the silver button down. The flame wavered on the stubby wick. "Why do you like my mother so much?" she asked, staring at the flame. "I hate her."

"Look at me, Iris."

"Just tell me why." She lit the corner of the Castle Bravo photograph. Yellow fire crawled toward her fingertips.

"What are you doing?"

She dropped the burning page into the wastebasket. Some of the chopped-off hair caught briefly, smoldered, and went out. "I'm mad at you."

"I thought we were friends," Louis said.

"Nope." Iris shook her head.

"Why not?"

"Because." Iris flipped the pages of the cloth-bound book to another glossy photograph of another mushroom cloud and ripped it out. "Because you like my mother and because you drank that stuff and because I hate everybody and because we're all going to die." She held the new page over the lighter.

"Stop that." Louis snatched the page from her hand. "We're not dying. There's no bombs." He held out his palm and she let the lighter fall into it. "I'll protect you," he said.

"You'd save my mother first." Iris narrowed her eyes at him. "Wouldn't you?"

He stared back, amazed at this rare interval of eye contact with Iris. Amazed at everything about her, the strange little girl who saw through everybody, understood everything, knew too much. He shoved the photo and the lighter into his pants pocket. "I'd save you both," he said. "No, I'd save you first."

"Why?" Iris plopped into the desk chair.

"Because we keep each other's secrets." Louis started gathering up the red plaid bedspread off the bed. "Now. Remember what I said?"

"What secrets?" Iris sat up straight and watched him.

He swirled the bedspread and struck a matador pose. "Remember? I said I knew how to cut hair."

"That's a secret?"

"That's one of them." He settled the spread around her shoulders and tucked it into her collar. "I'm pretty good, too. I needed money and I worked in a barbershop."

"It won't help now," she said.

"How do you know?"

"Because I'm a freak."

"No you're not." He combed his fingers experimentally through the hair at the back of Iris's head. "That's one of your secrets."

"What is?"

"Well, don't tell anyone." He picked up the paper doll scissors from the desk. "But you're going to be beautiful."

10

Family *Cucurbita*

I had known Rick for twenty minutes before he told me about his dead wife's uterus.

"Puerperal sepsis," he said, leaning on his garden spade. "Some of the placenta stayed in there after Angelica was born. It sort of rots and gets infected."

We were standing in my sad excuse for a vegetable garden. Behind Rick, over our low wall, I could see the professional-looking raised beds he was putting in his own backyard.

Rick told me how the infected uterus could have been treated in a hospital but they were living on Alaska's North Slope, along the Colville River, far from help. The baby was born during a six-day blizzard, the birth attended by an elderly Inupiaq woman who closed her eyes and keened when the wife's fever shot up.

Rick rambled on. "I worked as a bush pilot back then. Flew them out myself in the Staggerwing as soon as the weather cleared, but my wife died on the flight. Angelica was two days old." His eyes filled up. "That was March 14, 1972," he said, squinting back in time through fierce New Mexico sunlight.

Angelica, now five, played hopscotch behind us on Rick's patio. They had moved in two weeks ago, along with Rick's mother. That morning he had come over, introduced himself, and launched his life story with a brand of too-early intimacy that made me nervous. I was twenty-five, and my recently-wrecked relationships had made me wary of men, especially ones who teared up and talked placentas in the early going.

Rick swiped at his eyes. His fingernails were rimmed in garden dirt. His pink cheeks bloomed above his copper beard. He was a little over six feet, with a big barrel chest and big rounded shoulders. He had on a white t-shirt and overalls so large they looked like waders. Considering we had just met, he stood in too close and peered at me too intently, as if he were reading our conversation from subtitles on my forehead.

"Hannah," he said. "That's a beautiful name. Have you ever seen a Staggerwing?"

I hacked weakly at some star thistle with my hoe. "I don't think so." I wanted him to go back to his own garden where he belonged.

"It's a bi-plane. A classic. Mine was a Beech D17, built in 1945. The upper wing is inversely staggered behind the lower. She was beautiful. I wish I could've shown her to you. Do you live alone?"

"With my sister." I took another half-hearted swipe at the thistle. "Iris."

"Here, let me help you." Rick took the hoe out of my hands and made a vicious hack at the weed. To my delight, it still resisted. He upended the blade and grazed the edge with his thumb. "This needs sharpening. I can fix this for you." He held onto it, along with his spade, as if we were at a garage sale and he might buy them both. "What are you growing here?"

I hated people looking at my garden. I was stymied by the hard New Mexico dirt, despite consulting Horticultural Extension pamphlets about the hardiest plants to grow in the brutal Las Cruces summer. I bought faded packets of seed at Mondragon's Hardware-Septic-Nursery, amended the soil per instructions, and planted the seeds at the recommended depths. Now Rick eyed the broken plastic ruler I had stuck in the ground with a straightneck squash packet stapled on top. It was late April, already blazing hot, and nothing had come up yet. We stared at the bare earth as if new shoots might show themselves at any moment.

"I see you are interested in cucurbits," he said.

"Well, I thought I'd try some squash." I was already longing for the anonymity Iris and I had enjoyed over the past year while the next-door house had been up for sale. No one else on this Las Cruces block of chain-linked front yards and chained-up dogs and low stucco houses had paid any attention to us.

"Your gourds, your squashes, your pumpkins, those are all in the family Cucurbita," Rick said. "I'm fascinated by them too. Have you tested for phosphorus?"

"No. I just thought I'd see what happened."

"You've got to test for phosphorus!" he said. "I'm planning to put in pumpkins and the first thing I did was test for phosphorus. I could bring you my test kit."

"No thanks."

"It's not a problem. I'll bring it when I bring this back." He hefted my hoe and started across the driveway to his garage.

* * *

"What did Paul Bunyan want?" Iris asked. As I suspected, she had been watching from the kitchen window. Curious, but not willing to get involved.

What My Last Man Did

"Telling me about Mrs. Bunyan's infected uterus."

Iris dunked a raspberry leaf teabag in a cup. She sat at the kitchen table in her baggy shorts and baggy blouse, her white, skinny knees drawn up under her chin. Her dark-brown hair was tied in a ponytail with a purple rubber band off a Safeway bunch of broccoli. "Why does every man you meet immediately think of reproductive organs?"

"Good karma?" I knew she was going to bring up Quentin.

"The first day you met Quentin he asked if you wanted to see his penis."

"Iris, we were five."

"Still," she said. It was like this, living with someone who had total recall. You could name any date from Iris's twenty-seven-year life and she could tell you what happened that day. "You and Quentin *were* betrothed."

In a way, this was true. Our parents decided very early on that I would marry Quentin Boudreau McKenna, III. I liked Quentin, but I couldn't marry him. Instead I fled to Las Cruces and a job in the Chemistry Department of New Mexico State, where I started a romance with my boss. It fell apart three months later in an episode I'm sure has become department legend. Stockroom tryst, 12% solution hydrofluoric acid, bottle falling. The Grade 1 burns on his back required a trip to the ER and a confession to his wife. My job was gone, I was through with men, and I did not want Rick to like me.

"Paul Bunyan likes you," Iris said. "I could tell."

"How?"

"He was hovering. He was practically on top of you. He was trying to see down your blouse." Iris dunked her teabag, and perused one of the Horticultural Extension pamphlets, *You and Your Squash*.

"His name is Rick. He expounded on the family Cucurbita."

"You've got to love a man who knows his squash." Iris plopped the teabag in her saucer. "You should go out with him."

She always tossed out advice on things she didn't have to deal with. Happily cloistered with her studies and her writing, she left the real world to me. I admit I let it happen. I made her come and live with me after our mother sold our family home and its two hundred acres of Galveston Island and Iris went over the edge. When our mother died soon after, Iris mourned mainly the fact that the land and all its wildlife could have been saved if Mother had only kicked off a little sooner. We had both worshipped our father, and Iris did hold some esteem for our mother, who had recognized Iris's genius and allowed her to leave high school at fourteen to study by herself. This Iris had done nonstop for the past thirteen years.

* * *

Rick found an excuse almost every Saturday and Sunday to come over and join me in my garden. My soils were tested, my tools were sharpened, and the plastic ruler pieces were gone. Each row was marked with a tiny wooden billboard lovingly lettered in Rick's own hand. But by the first week of June, my squash had a serious case of powdery mildew. The fragile new leaves cringed and curled under mottled white splotches. I hated looking over at his raised beds with the giant pumpkin plants pushing their way out of the earth like alien life forms in a B movie.

One Sunday morning Rick brought his little girl, Angelica, with him. He also held in front of him, in the solemn manner of a wise man bearing gold, an orange box of fungicide. His garden-tool belt—with trowel, hand cultivator and weed digger swinging from their leather slots—clanked rhythmically on his waist. He had continued to fill me in on his autobiography and his many short-lived careers besides bush piloting, which included bus mechanic, oilrig roughneck, smokejumper and his current job as bricklayer for a construction company in Las Cruces.

He seemed to want an equally detailed résumé from me but I resisted, even though I had a comparable patchwork background of waitressing and grad school, fruit picking and teaching, typing and lab work. Where Rick glowed with pride at his versatility, I quailed with regret over my toe-in-the-water forays into jobs and relationships, my two degrees in chemistry that now felt meaningless. Still he pried. Were our parents alive? (No.) What had our father done? (Mining.) Good money in that? (Yes.)

"Angel, this is Hannah," he said to his daughter. "I want you two to get along."

Angelica twirled six rows of pearlescent pop-beads she wore on one wrist. She had on a Superman t-shirt and a skirt with a print of yellow light bulbs and green telephones. Her fine, white-blonde hair hung limply around her shoulders. "Can you say hi?" Rick asked.

"I have a pet tarantula," Angelica said. "Her name's Mabel."

"Really?"

"I have dirt in my sandals." She sat down and took off one white plastic sandal and shook it.

Above her head, Rick displayed the box of fungicide like a TV pitchman. "This stuff works on both anthracnose and powdery mildew."

"I don't like putting poisons on my plants," I said. I had tried a home remedy of vinegar and cayenne, but was too embarrassed to tell him. He looked at me as if I were a mother neglecting her children.

"But this will save your plants. I'll just give them a little." He started sprinkling the pellets around the plants.

"Please. I'd rather you didn't." I grabbed his arm and pulled. A big clump of pellets came out all at once spattered to the ground. Angelica sensed the danger. She scrambled to her feet and wandered over to our back door.

My hand was still on Rick's arm. He looked down on it, smiled, and covered it with his free hand. "You'll thank me," he said.

"Can I go in your house?" Angelica called. She was on our back step, both hands on the doorknob. Iris must have been watching again. The door suddenly opened and Angelica nearly fell inside. "Who are you?" Iris asked.

"I have a pet tarantula," Angelica said.

"Then you better come in." Iris pulled her in and shut the door.

"Was that your sister?" Rick asked. "Why doesn't she come out?"

"She's a little bit reclusive."

"I've been here a month and that's the first I've seen her. Is she sick?"

"She reads a lot."

Rick frowned at some chickweed springing up between rows of straightneck and crookneck squash. He unholstered his weed digger. "What does she read?" he asked, kneeling to tackle the chickweed.

"History. Science. She's working on a book. Several books, actually. One is about conquistadors."

"She reads and writes?" He made it sound like a miracle someone could do both.

"She's quite brilliant. Her IQ's 166."

Rick gathered up a green ball of chickweed and tossed it on the mulch pile. "So, are you two pretty well off?" he asked, as though he was tossing the question on the pile too.

"What?"

"Oh. I mean—" He pulled a folded white handkerchief from his pocket and shook it open as if to erase the question. "I just meant, are you supporting her? Do you work?"

It was true we had a hefty inheritance. Still I was half-heartedly looking for a job to justify all those years in school. When I didn't answer Rick's questions, he blew his nose—three deep honks—to fill the silence.

Iris and Angelica came outside. Angelica waved a book. "Daddy! Look what Iris gave me."

"What's that, Sweetie?"

"It's a book about spiders. There's a picture of Mabel!"

"*Brachypelma smithi*," Iris said.

"Mexican redknee tarantula," Angelica pronounced proudly, holding the book open to a glossy color plate of the spider. From the two hairy bulbs of its black and gray body, eight bristly legs jackknifed out in horrifying stripes of red, yellow and black.

Rick gently pried the book from Angelica's fingers. "We can't take this." He caressed the green cloth binding.

"Please, Daddy." Angelica peered up at him.

"Take it," Iris said. "She's very eager to learn."

Rick gave his daughter the book. "Can you say thank you?"

By way of thanks, Angelica hugged Iris's leg and buried her face in the wrinkled crotch of Iris's khaki shorts. Rick picked up his weed digger and the orange box of pellets. "Would you girls like to join us for supper next Saturday? My mother's been wanting to have you over."

"Say yes," Angelica begged, grabbing Iris's hand.

* * *

I was surprised Iris agreed to go to Rick's for dinner. But she had that reclusive person's curiosity about other people's lives, especially the interiors of their houses. She believed she could divine all their secrets from the patterns on their china, the fabrics of their bedspreads, and the sell-by dates on the spices in their kitchens. It was Saturday, and we were due at Rick's in an hour.

"I thought I might wear this." Iris held up a turquoise crinkle-cotton peasant skirt I didn't even know she owned. I wasn't sure

I had ever seen Iris in a skirt. Not since she was Little Bo-Peep in kindergarten. After kindergarten, Iris had jumped to third grade.

We were in her room. I was lying on her bed in the usual sea of books she slept with. Iris held the skirt against her waist, posing this way and that in the mirror, like a four-year-old playing dress-up. Finally she put on the skirt and a scoop-neck eyelet blouse that barely stayed up on her bony shoulders.

"I'm going as I am." I propped my feet on a copy of Aiton's *Antonio de Mendoza*. I was still in my jeans and NMSU Aggies t-shirt and had no intention of changing. If I made an effort, if I so much as put on lipstick or washed the dust out of my hair, I feared Rick would take it as encouragement.

"I think Mr. Bunyan is working up to asking you out." Iris brushed her hair hard, pulling it back from her face into a ponytail, then letting it drop and brushing again.

"No he's not," I said, though I feared she was right.

"Would you go?"

"No."

"Why not?"

"Because this is my year of no men." I picked up *Crónicas del Buenos Aires Colonial* and flipped through it, even though I did not read Spanish. Iris was fluent in Spanish and French.

"You haven't had a year of no men since junior high."

"I'm starting now."

* * *

Rick greeted us at his door looking scrubbed and eager, his beard freshly fluffed and his barrel chest bulging in a tie-dyed t-shirt of orange and magenta. We sat on his pumpkin-colored couch while he poured jelly-glass tumblers of blush wine from a jug. Iris admired two porcelain geisha figurines posing on the mantel with their parasols and rosebud lips. "They say geisha wore red undergarments to keep their reproductive organs healthy," she said. I gulped my wine, thinking of Rick's dead wife's reproductive organs, but he seemed unfazed as he refilled my glass. A stout woman in a light blue dress came in from the kitchen waving a wooden spoon and pushing frizzed gray hair off her forehead.

"This is Mona," Rick said. "My mother."

Mona's head seemed to balance like a bowling ball directly atop her sloping shelf of bosom. Her face glistened and her glasses were completely fogged. She tried to peer through them at Iris and me, her nose twitching as though she could identify us by scent.

"Is this the queer one?" She pointed the spoon at Iris. "The one who never leaves the house?"

"That's me!" Iris stuck out her hand, but Mona had already turned to me.

"Then you must be Hannah. I've heard all about you."

Angelica came in wearing a rhinestone tiara and a red cowgirl dress with white satin fringe down the arms. She carried a small aquarium that could only be the home of Mabel. I swigged more wine, while Iris rushed to greet the tarantula.

"She likes to show off her spider," Rick said.

"Isn't it dangerous?" I asked.

"No. They're quite docile and shy."

The aquarium appeared to be empty, except for some sticks and mossy-looking mounds of earth mixed with sawdust.

"Mabel hides a lot," Angelica said.

"*Brachypelma smithi* are burrowing spiders," Iris added. The two of them gazed expectantly into the aquarium.

We ate in the dining room on a mint-condition, gold-linoleum dinette set, circa 1952, with Mexican silver candelabra and a bowl of fat zucchini as a centerpiece. Mona padded heavily in and out from the kitchen on her dangerously swollen ankles, bearing Fiesta-ware platters of food made from recipes also frozen in 1952—frankfurter casserole topped with crumbled potato chips, creamed peas with pearl onions, and orange Jell-O that held suspended bits of canned pineapple and diced celery like insects trapped in amber. Angelica insisted on putting the aquarium on the table. Midmeal the mossy-looking earth stirred and Mabel's red- and yellow-striped legs poked into the air, where they waved and tentacled blindly before her entire hirsute body emerged, sloughing shreds of sawdust and dried grass.

"Look!" Angelica cried, as if we weren't already transfixed. She reached in and picked up the tarantula, which was twice the size of her five-year-old hand. I finished off my third glass of wine, trying to appear calm. Angelica offered the spider to Iris, who held out her cupped palms in the manner of a communicant receiving a wafer.

"She's beautiful," Iris said.

Mabel, for her part, sat motionless in Iris's hands, then sluggishly raised and lowered her jointed, hairy legs in a creepy ballet of eight-part grotesquery that took her a few tentative steps up Iris's arm.

"Angelica, put that thing away," Mona huffed.

Iris tilted her arm toward her plate, trying to interest the spider in her frankfurters. "Mabel, do you like processed animal products?"

"I mean it, child," Mona said.

"Come on, Mabel." Angelica retrieved the tarantula and plopped her back in the aquarium. Mabel began burrowing and quickly disappeared.

Dessert was lemon meringue pie that looked like it had been standing in the heat of the kitchen for a while. My gelatinous slab of meringue kept sliding off its gelatinous slab of lemon custard. Iris started cheerfully describing the bacteria that grew in room-temperature egg-whites.

"There's a group of *Salmonella enterica* that are subdivided by phage type," she said. "Enteritidis is the most common one for food poisoning." She went on to cover *Staphylococcus aureus* and the often-fatal *Clostridium botulinum*.

Rick forked pie into his mouth and listened closely. "Are you some kind of scientist?" he asked.

"No, I just like to read," Iris said.

After dessert, Mona cradled her head on the table and began to snore deeply. Iris made up a game with Angelica involving a world atlas and some crayons. In the kitchen I drank more wine and helped Rick with the dishes. By the time we left, I was embarrassingly drunk and Rick felt it necessary to guide Iris and me back to our front door. I went to my room, leaving them on the step discussing tarantulas and food-borne illness.

* * *

The following week I got a job at a medical testing lab doing comforting, mindless work. As I sat among the pap smears and PCB panels, I had plenty of time to reflect. The year of no men was not working out. I was starved for companionship, starved for sex, starved for something new. Even Rick was starting to look okay to me. In fact, he looked great compared to the yellow-complected head chemist who had asked me out on my first day of work. But if I got serious about any man, what would happen to Iris? She was all right with me around, but she still seemed so helpless. If she were living alone, I pictured her hunkering down in the house for years while it crumbled around her and she ate from the out-of-date jars of pimientos and anchovies that were shoved to the back of the pantry.

By mid-July, Rick's pellets had eradicated the powdery mildew, but the garden suffered under a plague of squash bugs. They had reduced the leaves to feathery gray doilies, and the budding straightnecks looked naked and afraid. While I stood in the hundred degree heat wondering if I should forget the whole enterprise,

Rick waved from his backyard where he strode between his luxuriant green plants in their perfectly groomed raised beds. I decided to run over there, rather than let him view the shame of the squash bugs. He ushered me into his garden like an elder letting a sinner back in church. Angelica was playing in her sandbox by the back steps. She always played alone but talked nonstop in strict, assertive tones, as if her imaginary friends required a lot of guidance.

Rick began a tour of the beds. "Costata romanesco," he said, fondling a heavy zucchini about to drop off its vine. "They're the best eating. These are Embassies." He waved off the less-impressive zucchini and moved on. He had beautiful Sierra Blanca onions, as well as a new hybrid called Numex José Fernández. He saved the pumpkin beds for last. The bulbous orange vegetables reclined this way and that all over the ground, inviting and obscene, like bored hookers in a whorehouse. I read the varieties off the row labels: Oktoberfest, Cinderella, Sorcerer.

"These are your ribs." Rick knelt to indicate between thumb and forefinger the longitudinal sections of a Cinderella pumpkin. "You want good rib definition and good rib uniformity." The pumpkin, lounging there in the blazing heat of his garden, radiated carotene and vitality under the caress of his fingertips. "The handle's important too." He slid his hand from the ribs to the fat green stem and grasped it in a vaguely sexual way. "A weak handle can be a sign of overall malaise, or too much fertilizer." He rocked the pumpkin gently by the handle. "This one's nice and stiff."

Angelica came up behind us. "Where is Iris?" she demanded.

"She's inside," I said.

"Can I get her?" Angelica didn't wait for an answer, but trotted toward our house.

"I've got a little secret," Rick said. He stood up and dropped a conspiratorial paw on my shoulder, as if we were comrades in the pumpkin underground. "I'm going to enter one of these Cinderellas in the Doña Ana County Fair. Wish me luck."

"That's great." I felt a surprising twist of jealousy in my chest. "Why is it a secret?"

Rick looked offended that I should question the clandestine aspect of his plan. "Their cucurbit competition is quite extensive," he said, as if that explained it.

Angelica and Iris came over, hand in hand.

"Daddy, Iris is going to teach me about the birds," Angelica called out. "She knows everything." I was surprised to see that Angelica had Iris's nine-hundred-dollar Zeiss-Ikon binoculars hanging around her neck. She scanned a Chinese elm for sparrows. Iris looked at the pumpkins. "These are beautiful," she said. "The ribs are so well-defined."

"Daddy's going to enter a contest," Angelica announced.

* * *

By August, I was ready to give up on the garden. Not wanting to abandon the plants entirely to the full fury of the summer sun, I continued to water most mornings, muttering encouragement to my valiant, all-but-defeated cucurbits. A few plants struggled to maturity. I struggled with questions about where life was taking me. Why was I wasting time in a dead-end job? Why was my past full of men I couldn't hang on to? Why was I letting Iris depend on me when she should be getting out on her own? Had I been too hard on Rick? When I thought about it, he had a good heart and he was gentle and loving with Angelica. Maybe one of my answers was right next door. Meanwhile, I turned to home improvement on the weekends. I painted the kitchen cabinets and installed fancy wrought-iron curtain rods and new drapes throughout the house. On the second Saturday in September, I was laying a new tile backsplash in the bathroom when a knock came at the front screen door.

It was Rick. He looked overheated in a suit and tie—the temperature was in the nineties—and had a green canvas backpack on his back. In his arms he held a gigantic, glowing pumpkin with a stout green handle.

I opened the screen and he strode in, set the pumpkin on the coffee table, took off the backpack and his jacket, and sat down, hands on knees, as if we had a scheduled appointment.

"Rick—" He held up a hand to silence me and drew from the backpack a foot-long blue satin ribbon. He propped it against the pumpkin, trying to look proud and humble at the same time.

"Congratulations," I said. The top of the ribbon was a ruffled blue button with gold lettering: *First Place—Mid-Size Pumpkins—Doña Ana County Fair 1977.*

"Is Iris here?"

"She's at the library, Rick, but I'm sure she'll be happy for you too."

"Actually, I saw her leave," Rick admitted. "I wanted to talk to you."

I froze. I had known this was coming. I had thought about it for a month, and I still had no idea what I wanted. At least I could stall with the truth. "Rick, right at this moment, I'm laying tile. I've got adhesive spread all over the bathroom."

"Latex-modified or dry-set?" he asked.

"I don't know. It's just something I got at Mondragon's."

"I could've helped you with that." Rick pulled a cardboard folder stuffed with papers from the backpack and placed it on his knees. "I know you and Iris have lost your parents," he began.

"Rick—"

"Please, hear me out. I'm just an old-fashioned guy and I want to do things right."

"What things?"

"Well, you're the closest relative Iris has, so I felt I should ask you first."

"Ask me what?"

"For permission. To court her. To 'pursue' Iris." He put fingertip quotation marks around "pursue." His fingernails were still dark with garden dirt.

My whole brain rolled over like one of those screens at the airport displaying all new arrival times for delayed flights. "That's very . . . kind of you. . . ."

"I have great admiration for Iris. And Angelica loves her."

My eyes went to the folder on his lap.

"Oh," he said. "I didn't want you to think I was taking advantage. Financial advantage, I mean. I brought some of my portfolio."

He opened the folder and a few papers slid to the floor. Others spilled out on the coffee table. "The bankers call it a portfolio. I just call it my money." He showed me some statements that looked a lot like the ones the bankers and lawyers were always sending Iris and me. "When I sold the Staggerwing and my other airplanes, I made some good investments." He pointed with a pen at some columns I had no interest in reading.

The screen door squeaked open and Iris came in with an armload of books. Her gaze went from the pumpkin to the ribbon to Rick.

"You won?" She knelt by the coffee table, dropped her books, and sort of embraced the pumpkin.

"Iris, Rick has come to ask my permission to pursue you in courtship." I was worried how she would handle this, but I couldn't protect her now. "Isn't that sweet?"

Iris put her cheek against one of the well-defined ribs. "It's warm," she said.

"Is that a yes?" Rick asked.

* * *

Rick and Iris were married two months later. They left on a trip to Mazatlán with Angelica and Mona in tow. Near dusk on a

November day, I wandered into the garden to turn over the dead squash plants and cover the beds for winter. I found one of the discarded, desiccated straightnecks that had died early in the summer. The pale ivory oval fit in my hand. I tossed it aside and made a few more half-hearted stabs with my spade. A cottonwood leaf beetle scuttled out of the loosened earth, frantic legs working the sandy dirt, orange and black body desperate for a new hiding place. The sunset was fading, and an ocher moon pushed its way into the dark blue sky.

Credits

"Rancho Cielito" appeared in *Ontario Review*, No. 65, Fall/Winter 2006–07.

"What My Last Man Did" appeared in *Harpur Palate*, Volume 7 No. 2, Winter 2008.

"Tierra Blanca" appeared in *Bryant Literary Review*, Volume 11, 2010.

"Family Cucurbita" appeared in *The MacGuffin*, Volume XXVII No. 1, Fall 2010.

"Do Nothing Till You Hear From Me" appeared in *Cold Mountain Review*, Volume 40 No. 2, Spring 2012.

"The Empire Pool" appeared in *Conclave*, Issue 5, Spring, 2013.

"Tchoupitoulas" appeared in *Prairie Schooner*, Volume 89 No. 1, Spring, 2015.

ANDREA LEWIS's stories, essays and prose poems have appeared in *Prairie Schooner, Catamaran Literary Reader, Cutthroat,* and many other literary journals. She lives with her husband on Vashon Island, Washington. She is a founding member of Richard Hugo House, a place for writers in Seattle.

CPSIA information can be obtained
at www.ICGtesting.com
Printed in the USA
LVOW12s1735160317
527463LV00003B/752/P